JESSICA ABEL

TRISH TRASH

❶ ❷ ❸

TRASH

ROLLERGIRL OF MARS

By Jessica Abel

Backgrounds and Design
Lydia Roberts

Colors
Walter

SUPER GENIUS

New York

JESSICA ABEL
TRISH ❶ ❷ ❸ TRASH
ROLLERGIRL OF MARS

Backgrounds and design by Lydia Roberts
Colors by Walter

Super Genius books may be purchased for
business or promotional use. For information
on bulk purchases please contact Macmillan
Corporate and Premium Sales Department at
(800) 221-7945 x 5442

Super Genius graphic novels are also
available digitally wherever e-books are sold.

Super Genius is an imprint of Papercutz.

JayJay Jackson — Production
Jeff Whitman — Editor
Jim Salicrup
Editor-in-Chief

ISBN: 978-1-5458-0016-4

Printed in China
October 2018

Distributed by Macmillan
First Printing

To Kim Stanley Robinson for taking me on my first trip to Mars.

Our Story So Far...

Seven-and-a-half-year-old (that's fifteen in Earth years), Patricia "Trish Trash" Nupindju is a talented young hoverderby player on Mars 200 years in the future. Too young to go pro with her local team, the Terror Novas, she accepts an unpaid internship as the team's "skategirl." It seems like the only way to escape a future of poverty and hard labor on her aunt and uncle's moisture farm in Candor Chasma, where they work as indentured labor for the Arex Corporation.

When she encounters Qiqi, an indigenous Martian "bug," out in the rough near her farmhouse, Trish provides shelter and gains an ally. Qiqi presents Trish and best friend Marq with gifts that can change everything: organic skates to get an advantage on the rink and lichen that can revolutionize moisture farming...

The future is bright but dangerous. Trish's tio accepted a risky Temporary Labor Assignment to help pay off family debt, leaving Trish and her aunt exposed with thier newfound fortune in water, and Arex is sniffing around.

TRISH TRASH # 1

TRISH TRASH # 2

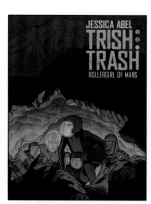
TRISH TRASH # 3

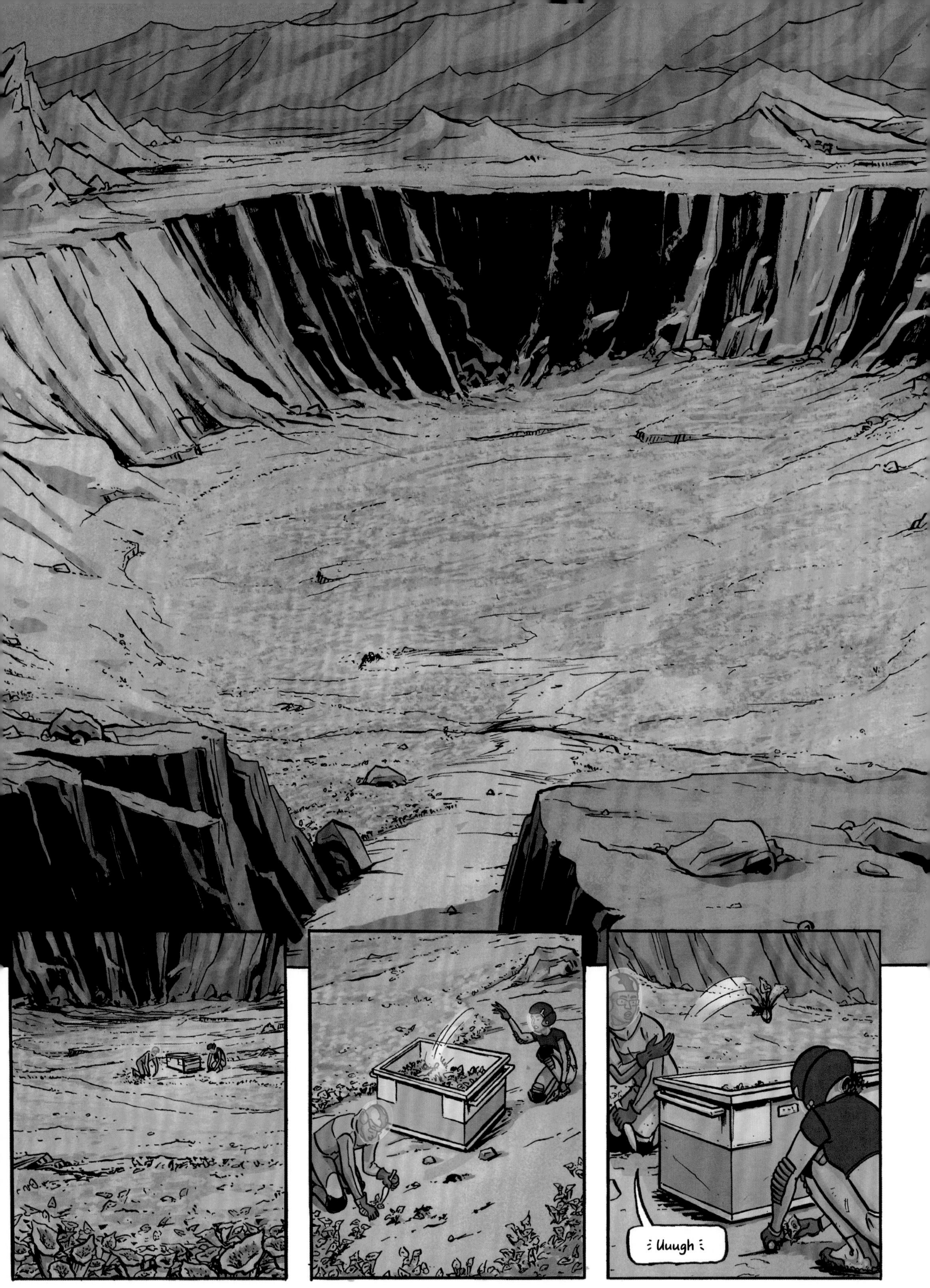
Uuugh

Oh, my back.

Hey, help me with this side. The forward hoverpad is dusted, but I don't have time to fix it.

Where is Rocky today?

She's got an early practice. Team is slipping.

Well, that's obviously a good use of her time.

Lay off, Marq. They've got a shot at the Derby Bowl if they get back on track.

Which will definitely change her life more than having a whole bunch of water.

Let me put this in terms you'll understand: she's under contract.

Pff

Hey, young moisture farmers of Mars! It's your old pal Marquis Marq with a cheerful message of motivation!

Are you doing your stupid political holog again?

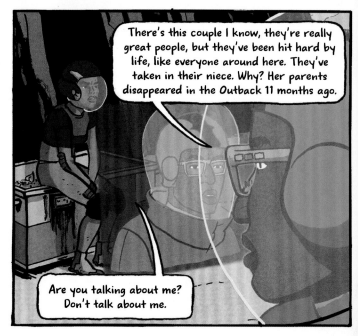

There's this couple I know, they're really great people, but they've been hit hard by life, like everyone around here. They've taken in their niece. Why? Her parents disappeared in the Outback 11 months ago.

Are you talking about me? Don't talk about me.

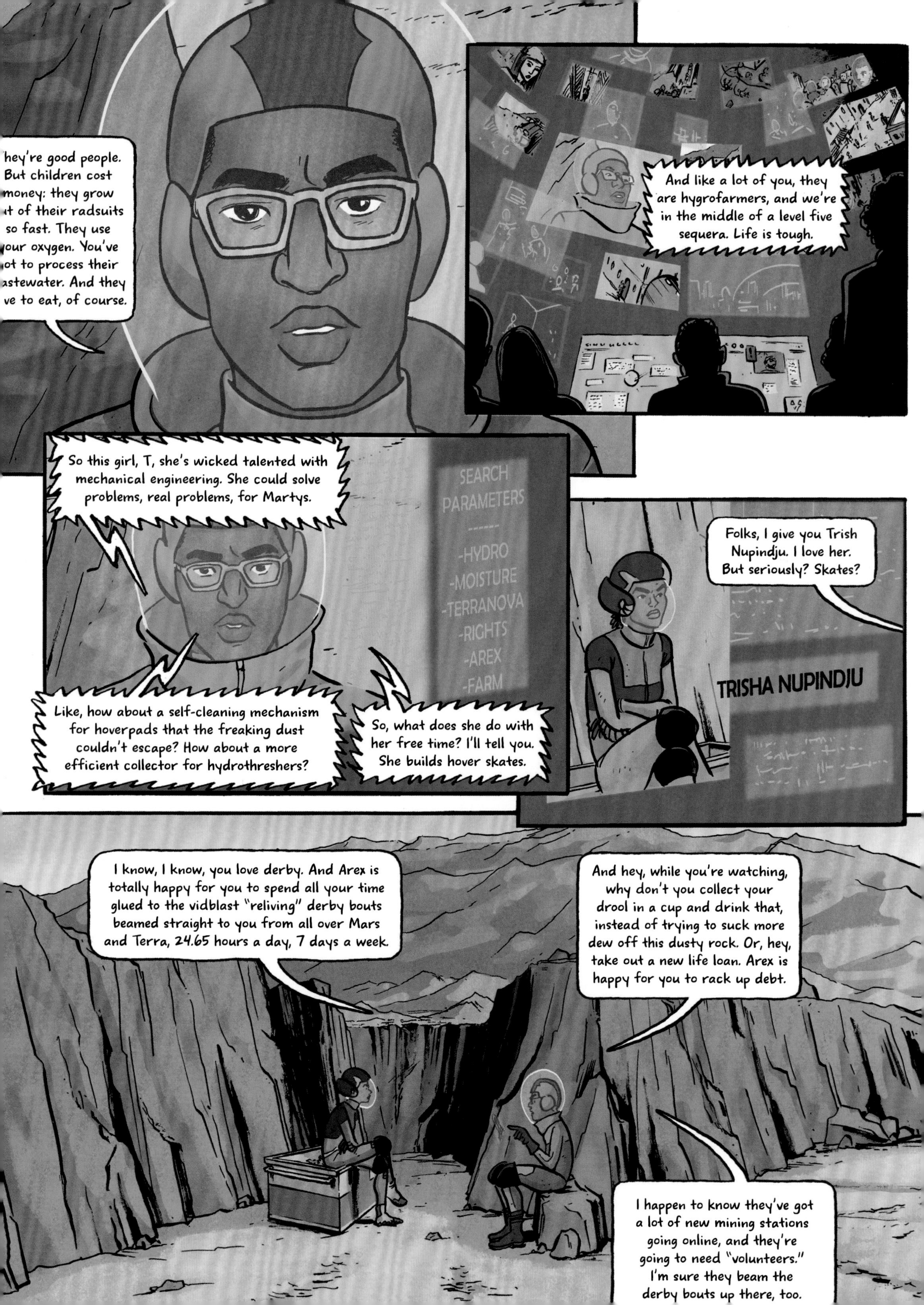
hey're good people. But children cost money: they grow ıt of their radsuits so fast. They use your oxygen. You've ıot to process their astewater. And they ve to eat, of course.
And like a lot of you, they are hygrofarmers, and we're in the middle of a level five sequera. Life is tough.
So this girl, T, she's wicked talented with mechanical engineering. She could solve problems, real problems, for Martys.
SEARCH PARAMETERS
-HYDRO
-MOISTURE
-TERRANOVA
-RIGHTS
-AREX
-FARM
Like, how about a self-cleaning mechanism for hoverpads that the freaking dust couldn't escape? How about a more efficient collector for hydrothreshers?
So, what does she do with her free time? I'll tell you. She builds hover skates.
Folks, I give you Trish Nupindju. I love her. But seriously? Skates?
TRISHA NUPINDJU
I know, I know, you love derby. And Arex is totally happy for you to spend all your time glued to the vidblast "reliving" derby bouts beamed straight to you from all over Mars and Terra, 24.65 hours a day, 7 days a week.
And hey, while you're watching, why don't you collect your drool in a cup and drink that, instead of trying to suck more dew off this dusty rock. Or, hey, take out a new life loan. Arex is happy for you to rack up debt.
I happen to know they've got a lot of new mining stations going online, and they're going to need "volunteers." I'm sure they beam the derby bouts up there, too.

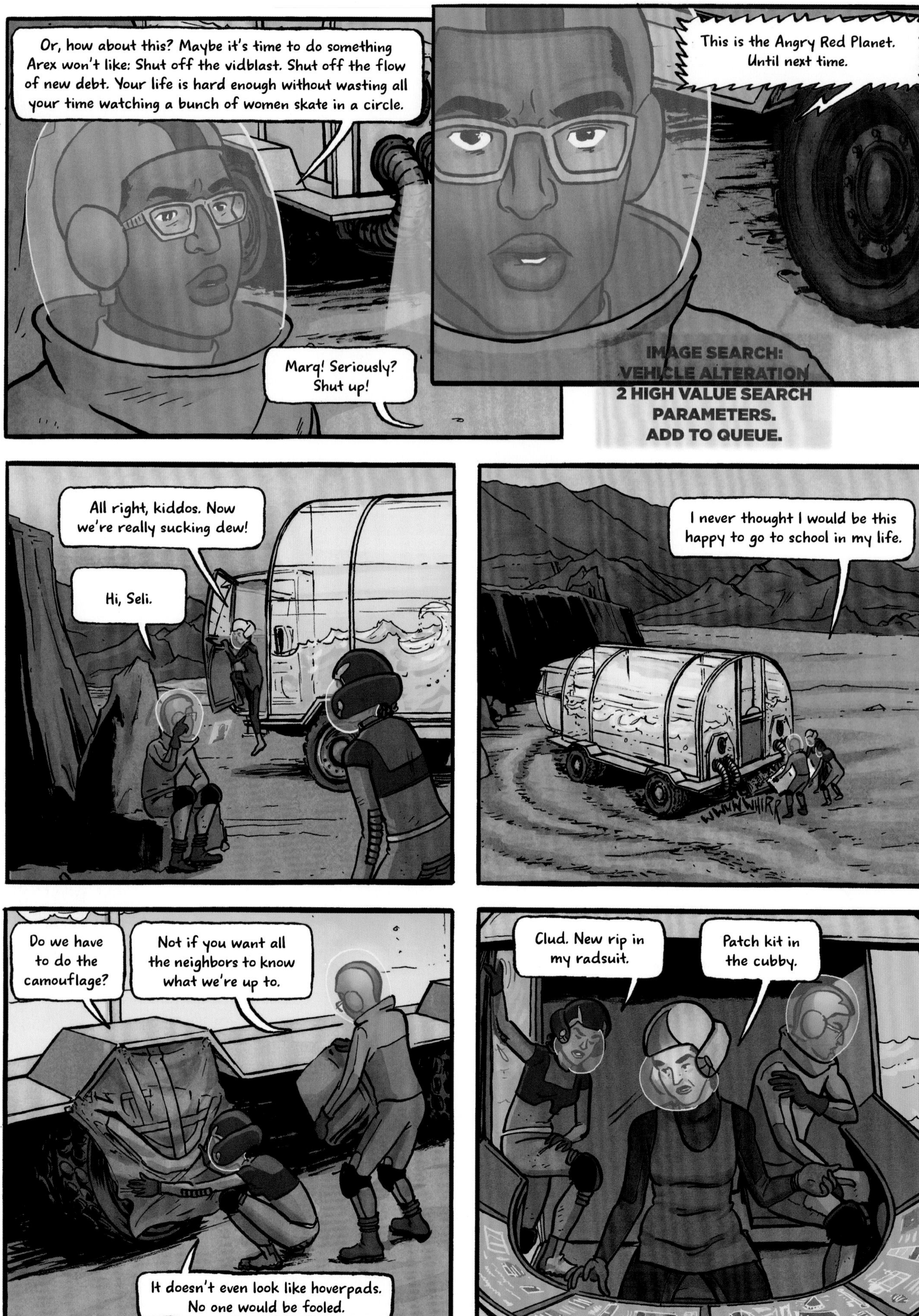
Or, how about this? Maybe it's time to do something Arex won't like: Shut off the vidblast. Shut off the flow of new debt. Your life is hard enough without wasting all your time watching a bunch of women skate in a circle.
Marq! Seriously? Shut up!
This is the Angry Red Planet. Until next time.
IMAGE SEARCH: VEHICLE ALTERATION
2 HIGH VALUE SEARCH PARAMETERS. ADD TO QUEUE.
All right, kiddos. Now we're really sucking dew!
Hi, Seli.
I never thought I would be this happy to go to school in my life.
WWWWWHIRR
Do we have to do the camouflage?
Not if you want all the neighbors to know what we're up to.
It doesn't even look like hoverpads. No one would be fooled.
Clud. New rip in my radsuit.
Patch kit in the cubby.

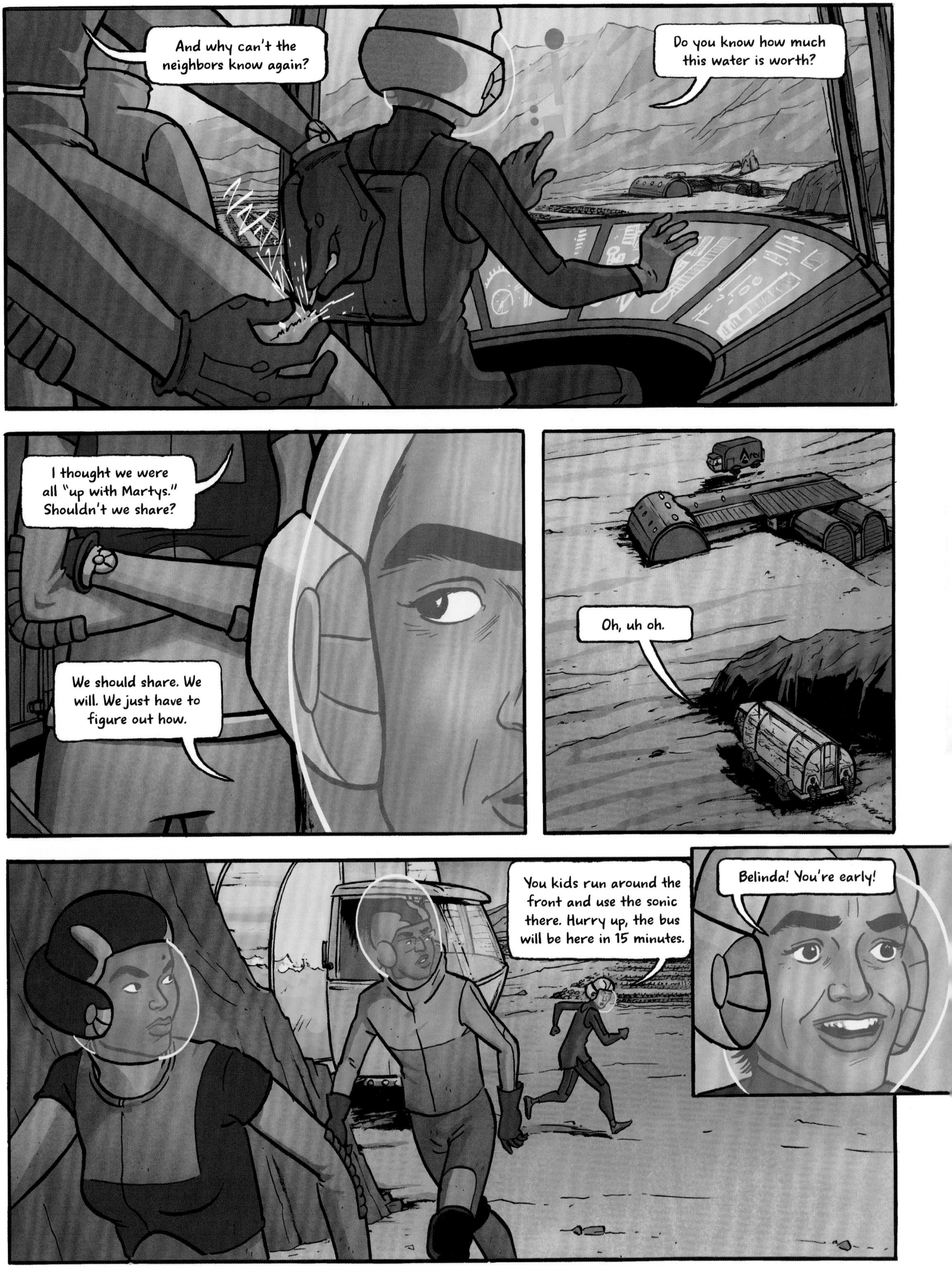
And why can't the neighbors know again?
Do you know how much this water is worth?
I thought we were all "up with Martys." Shouldn't we share?
We should share. We will. We just have to figure out how.
Oh, uh oh.
You kids run around the front and use the sonic there. Hurry up, the bus will be here in 15 minutes.
Belinda! You're early!

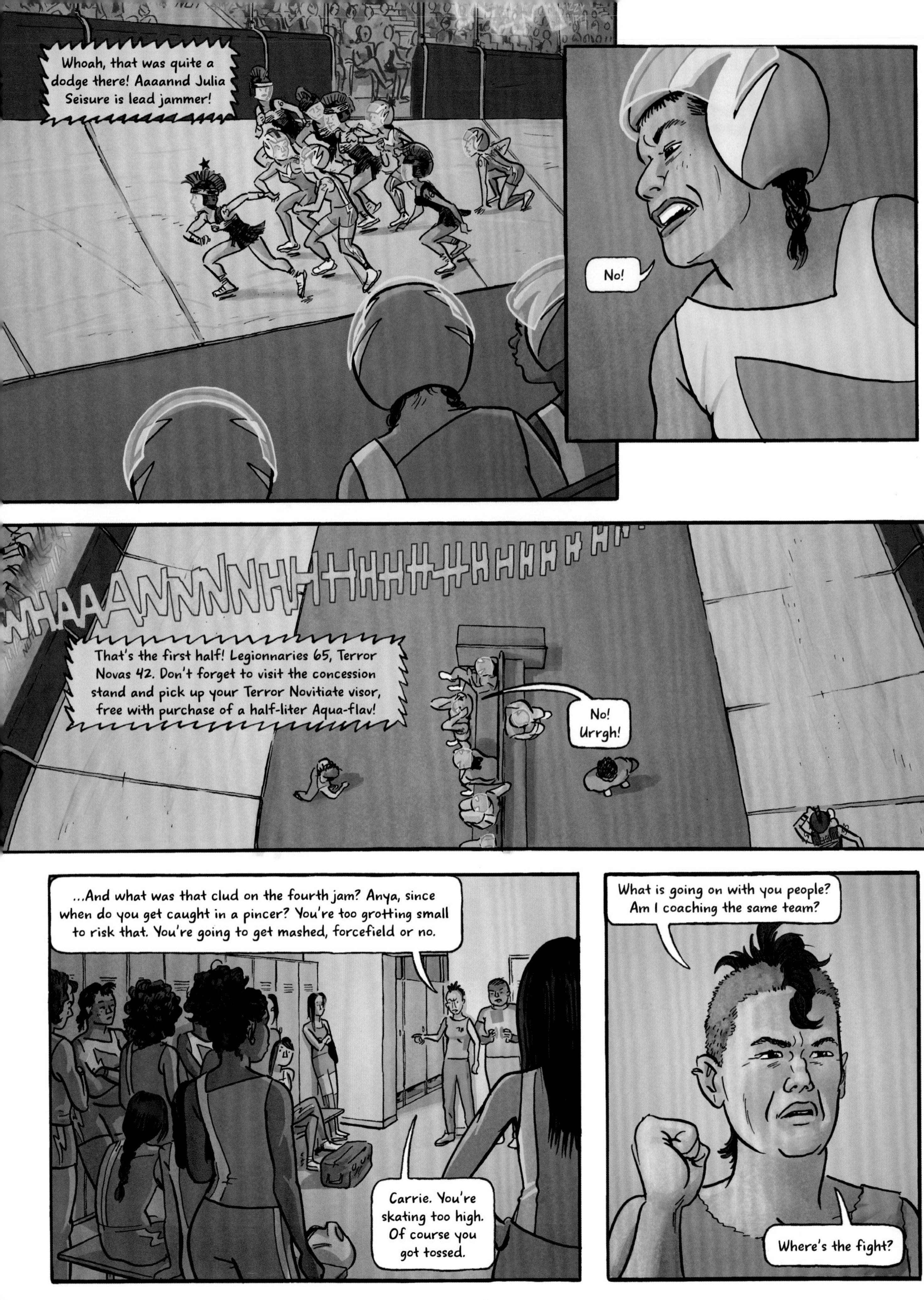
Whoah, that was quite a dodge there! Aaaannd Julia Seisure is lead jammer!
No!
WHAAANNNNNHHHHHHHHHHHHHHHHHH
That's the first half! Legionnaries 65, Terror Novas 42. Don't forget to visit the concession stand and pick up your Terror Novitiate visor, free with purchase of a half-liter Aqua-flav!
No! Urrgh!
...And what was that clud on the fourth jam? Anya, since when do you get caught in a pincer? You're too grotting small to risk that. You're going to get mashed, forcefield or no.
Carrie. You're skating too high. Of course you got tossed.
What is going on with you people? Am I coaching the same team?
Where's the fight?

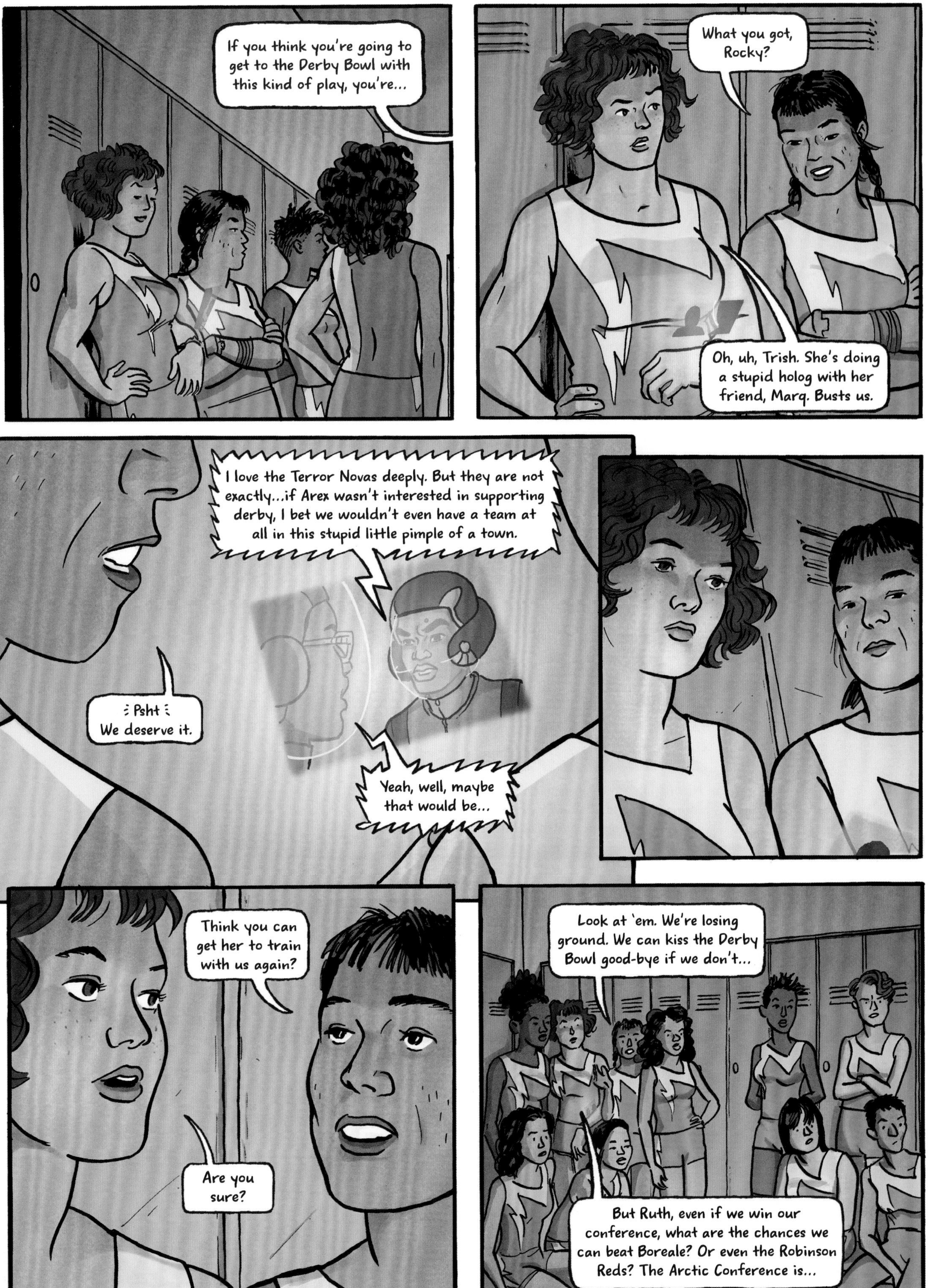
If you think you're going to get to the Derby Bowl with this kind of play, you're...
What you got, Rocky?
Oh, uh, Trish. She's doing a stupid holog with her friend, Marq. Busts us.
I love the Terror Novas deeply. But they are not exactly...if Arex wasn't interested in supporting derby, I bet we wouldn't even have a team at all in this stupid little pimple of a town.
Psht
We deserve it.
Yeah, well, maybe that would be...
Think you can get her to train with us again?
Are you sure?
Look at 'em. We're losing ground. We can kiss the Derby Bowl good-bye if we don't...
But Ruth, even if we win our conference, what are the chances we can beat Boreale? Or even the Robinson Reds? The Arctic Conference is...

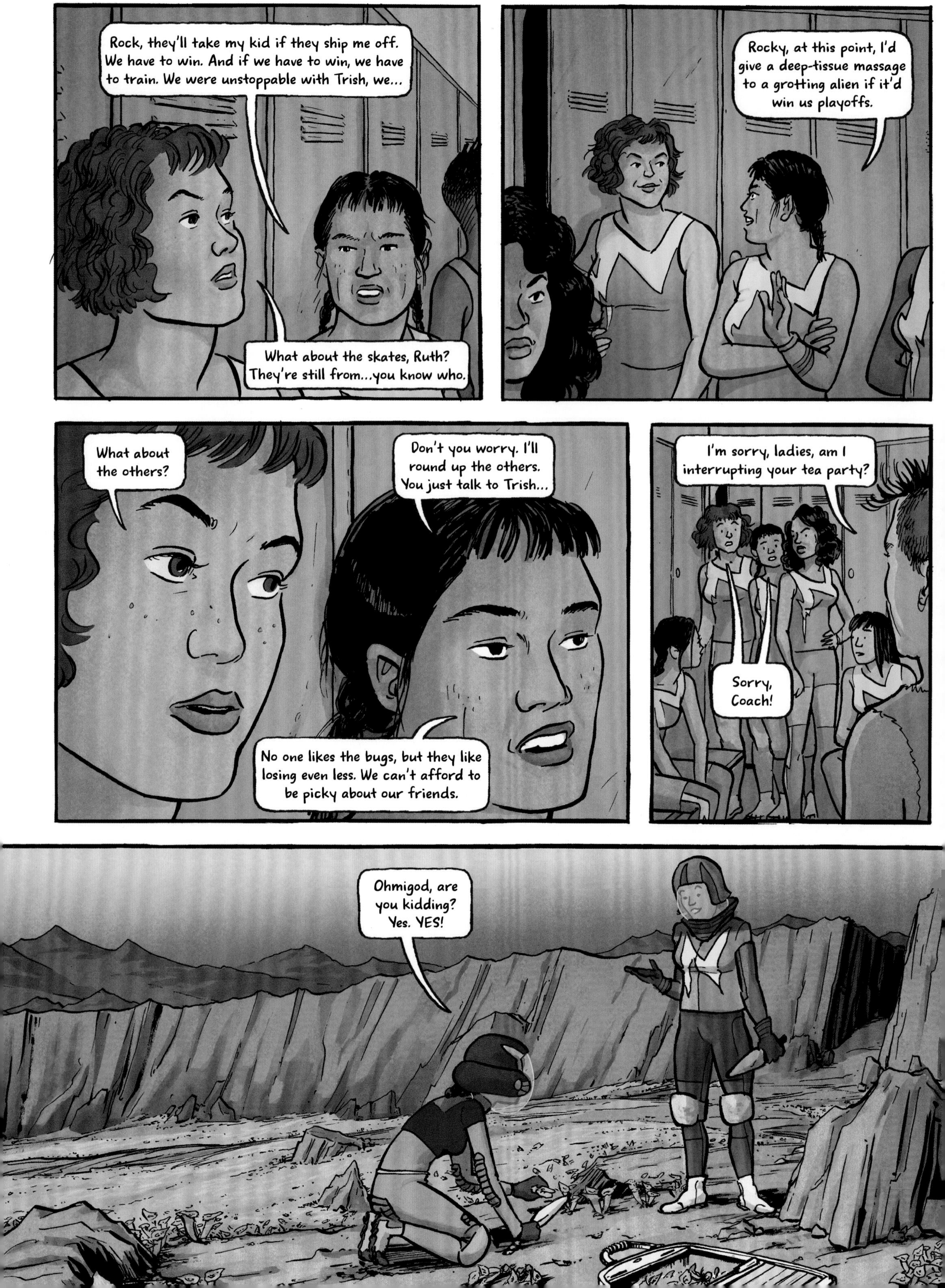

Rock, they'll take my kid if they ship me off. We have to win. And if we have to win, we have to train. We were unstoppable with Trish, we...
What about the skates, Ruth? They're still from...you know who.
Rocky, at this point, I'd give a deep-tissue massage to a grotting alien if it'd win us playoffs.
What about the others?
Don't you worry. I'll round up the others. You just talk to Trish...
No one likes the bugs, but they like losing even less. We can't afford to be picky about our friends.
I'm sorry, ladies, am I interrupting your tea party?
Sorry, Coach!
Ohmigod, are you kidding? Yes. YES!

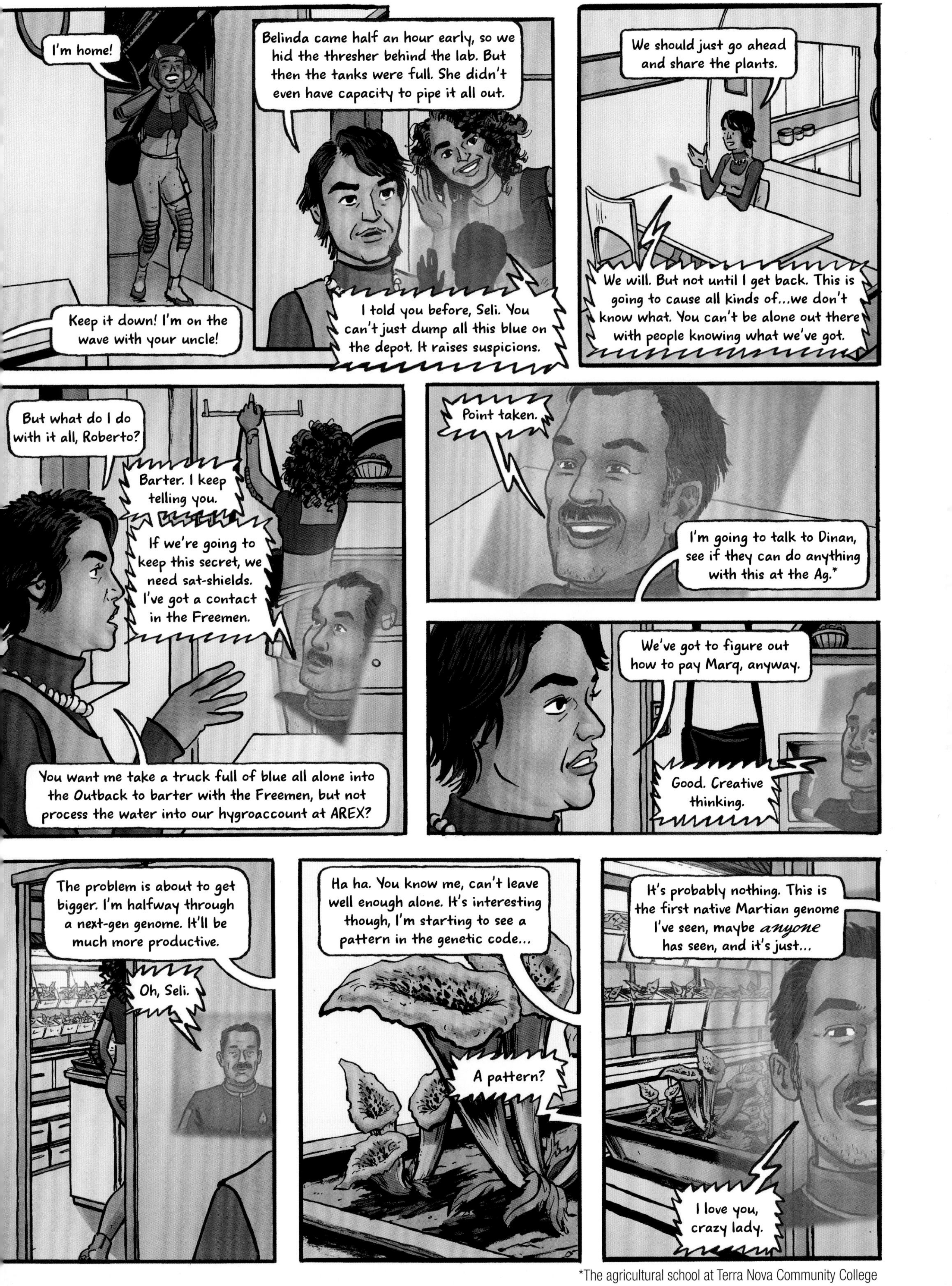
I'm home!
Keep it down! I'm on the wave with your uncle!
Belinda came half an hour early, so we hid the thresher behind the lab. But then the tanks were full. She didn't even have capacity to pipe it all out.
I told you before, Seli. You can't just dump all this blue on the depot. It raises suspicions.
We should just go ahead and share the plants.
We will. But not until I get back. This is going to cause all kinds of...we don't know what. You can't be alone out there with people knowing what we've got.
But what do I do with it all, Roberto?
Barter. I keep telling you.
If we're going to keep this secret, we need sat-shields. I've got a contact in the Freemen.
You want me take a truck full of blue all alone into the Outback to barter with the Freemen, but not process the water into our hygroaccount at AREX?
Point taken.
I'm going to talk to Dinan, see if they can do anything with this at the Ag.*
We've got to figure out how to pay Marq, anyway.
Good. Creative thinking.
The problem is about to get bigger. I'm halfway through a next-gen genome. It'll be much more productive.
Oh, Seli.
Ha ha. You know me, can't leave well enough alone. It's interesting though, I'm starting to see a pattern in the genetic code...
A pattern?
It's probably nothing. This is the first native Martian genome I've seen, maybe *anyone* has seen, and it's just...
I love you, crazy lady.

*The agricultural school at Terra Nova Community College

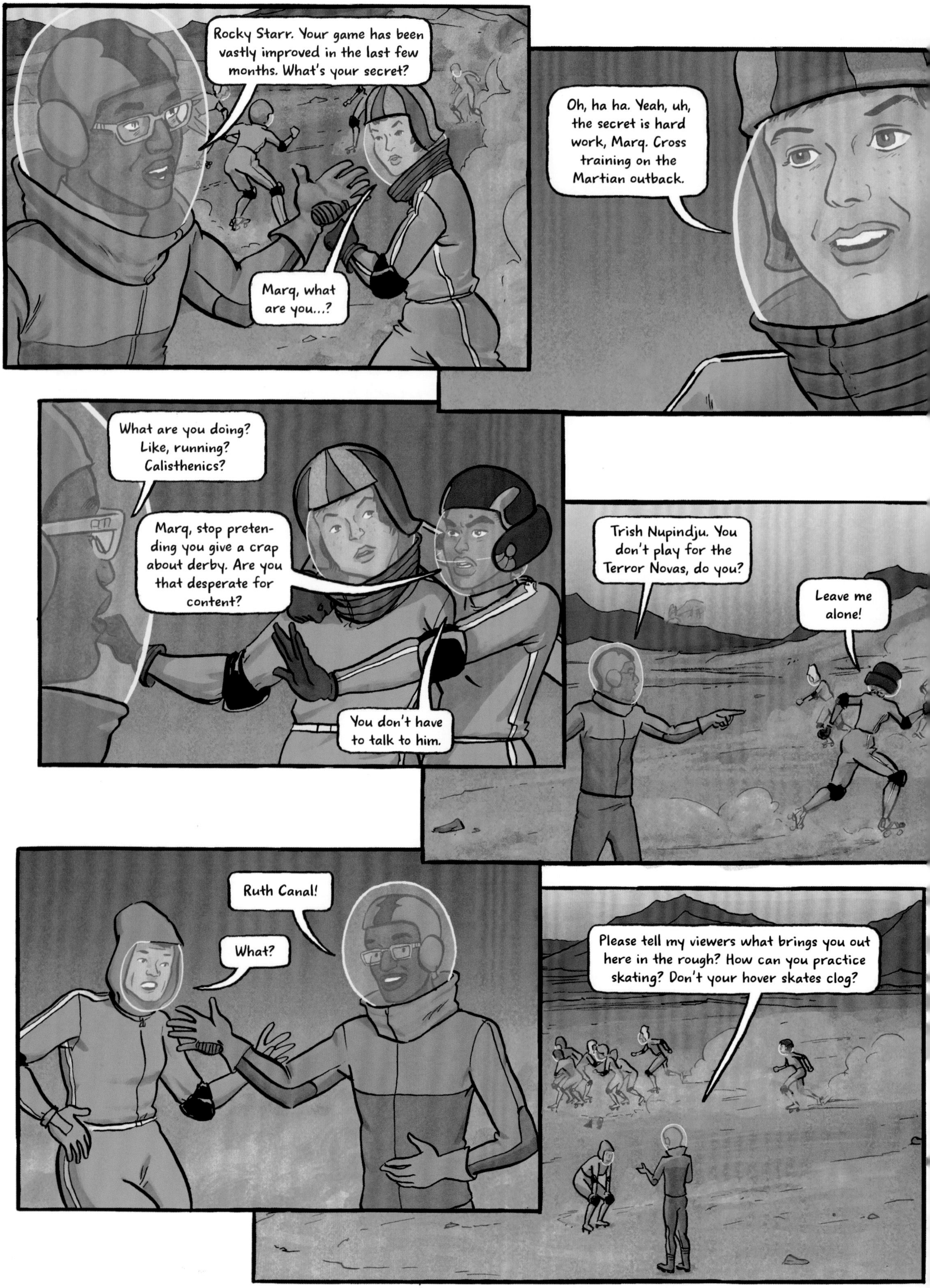
Rocky Starr. Your game has been vastly improved in the last few months. What's your secret?
Marq, what are you...?
Oh, ha ha. Yeah, uh, the secret is hard work, Marq. Cross training on the Martian outback.
What are you doing? Like, running? Calisthenics?
Marq, stop pretending you give a crap about derby. Are you that desperate for content?
You don't have to talk to him.
Trish Nupindju. You don't play for the Terror Novas, do you?
Leave me alone!
Ruth Canal!
What?
Please tell my viewers what brings you out here in the rough? How can you practice skating? Don't your hover skates clog?

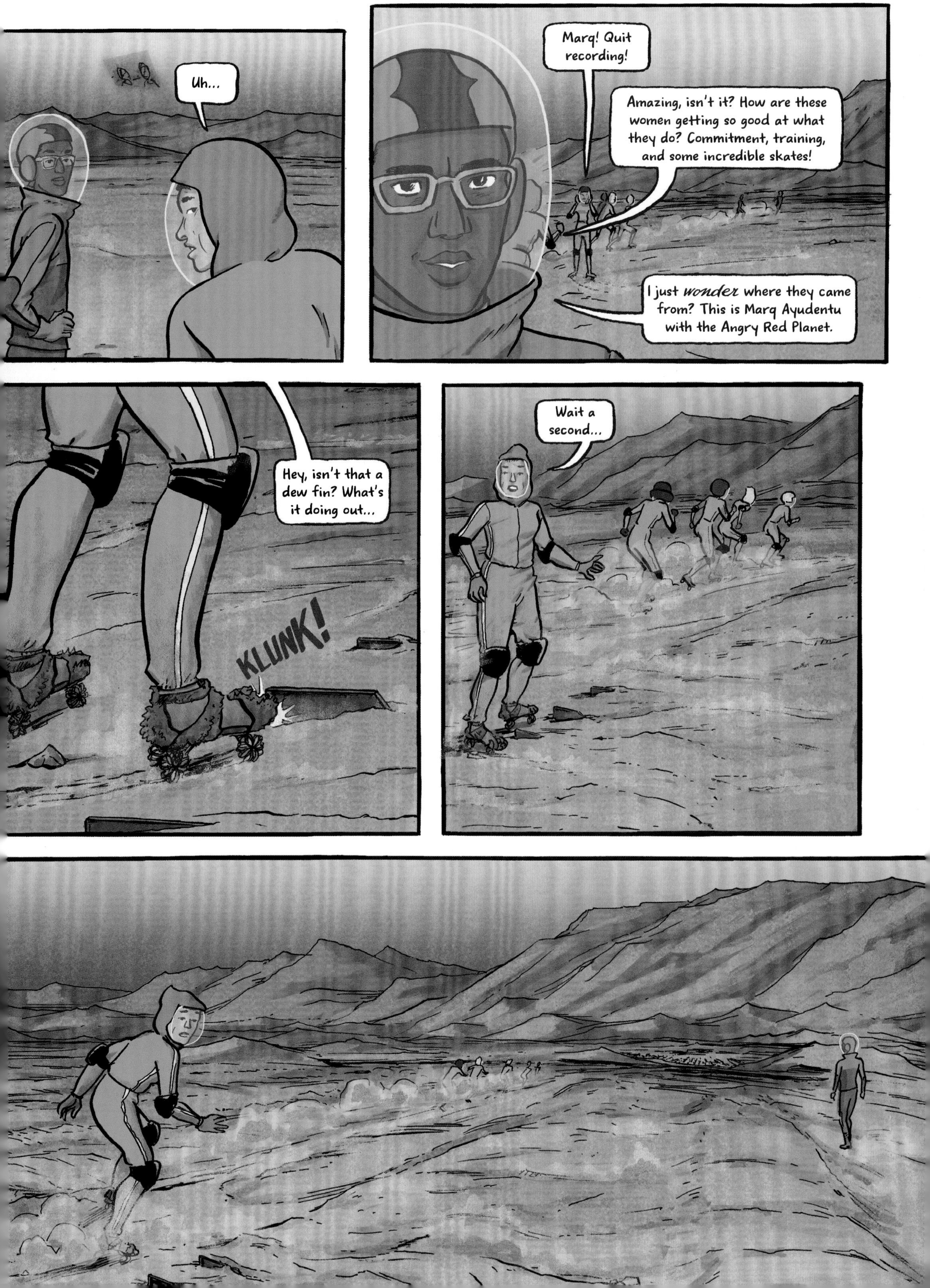
Uh...
Marq! Quit recording!
Amazing, isn't it? How are these women getting so good at what they do? Commitment, training, and some incredible skates!
I just *wonder* where they came from? This is Marq Ayudentu with the Angry Red Planet.
Hey, isn't that a dew fin? What's it doing out...
KLUNK!
Wait a second...

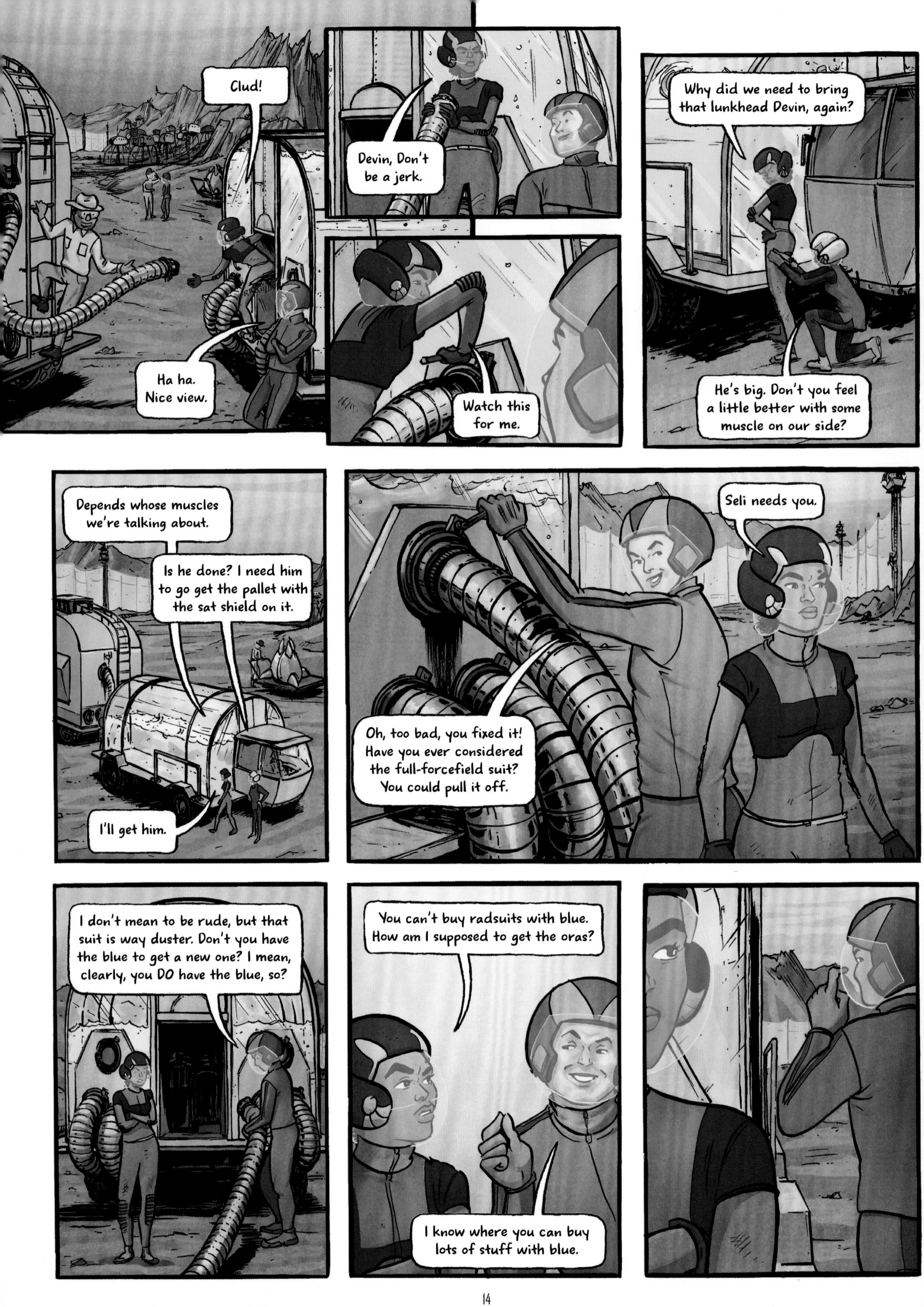

Clud!
Ha ha. Nice view.
Devin, Don't be a jerk.
Watch this for me.
Why did we need to bring that lunkhead Devin, again?
He's big. Don't you feel a little better with some muscle on our side?
Depends whose muscles we're talking about.
Is he done? I need him to go get the pallet with the sat shield on it.
I'll get him.
Seli needs you.
Oh, too bad, you fixed it! Have you ever considered the full-forcefield suit? You could pull it off.
I don't mean to be rude, but that suit is way duster. Don't you have the blue to get a new one? I mean, clearly, you DO have the blue, so?
You can't buy radsuits with blue. How am I supposed to get the oras?
I know where you can buy lots of stuff with blue.

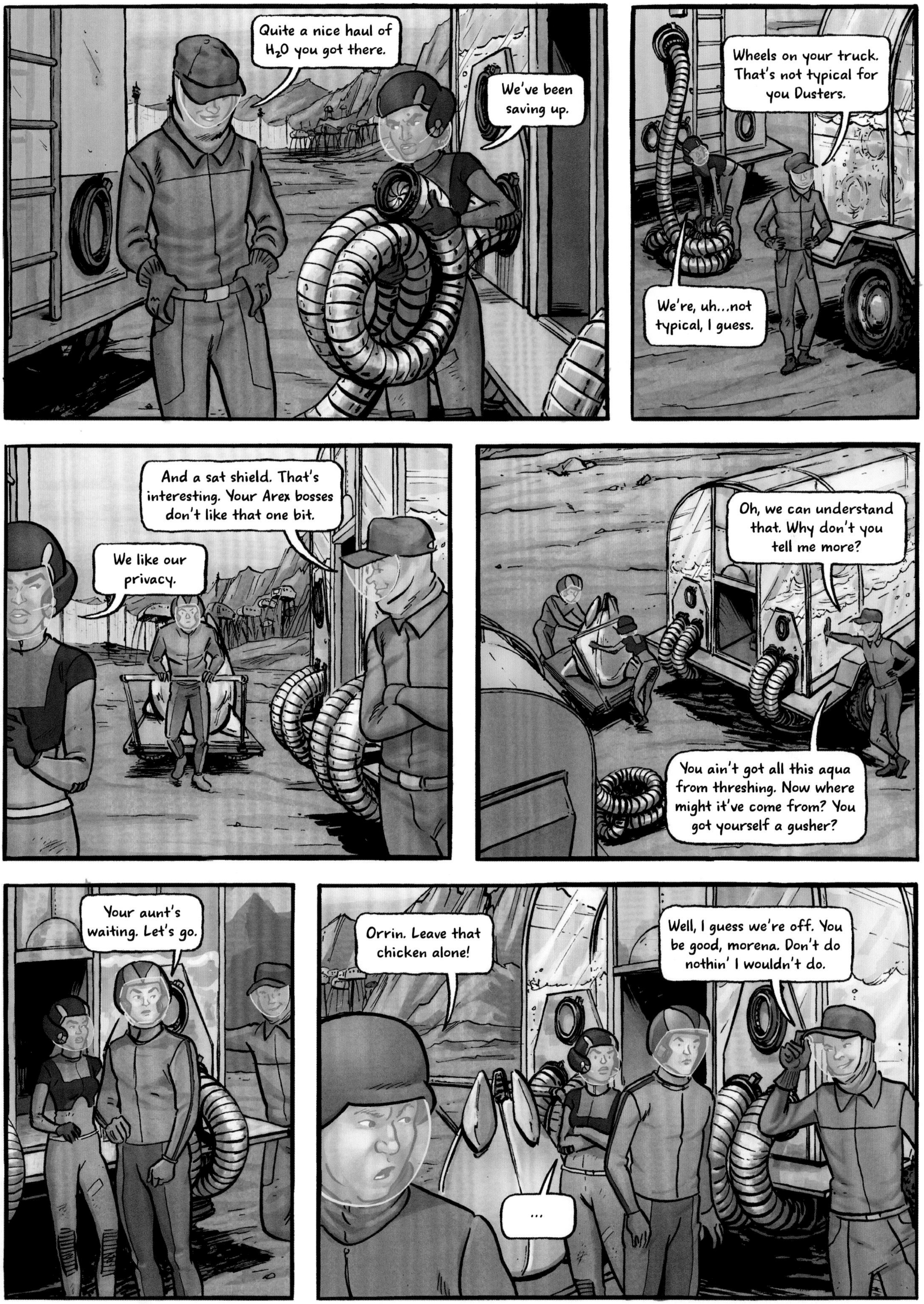

Quite a nice haul of H_2O you got there.
We've been saving up.
Wheels on your truck. That's not typical for you Dusters.
We're, uh...not typical, I guess.
And a sat shield. That's interesting. Your Arex bosses don't like that one bit.
We like our privacy.
Oh, we can understand that. Why don't you tell me more?
You ain't got all this aqua from threshing. Now where might it've come from? You got yourself a gusher?
Your aunt's waiting. Let's go.
Orrin. Leave that chicken alone!
...
Well, I guess we're off. You be good, morena. Don't do nothin' I wouldn't do.

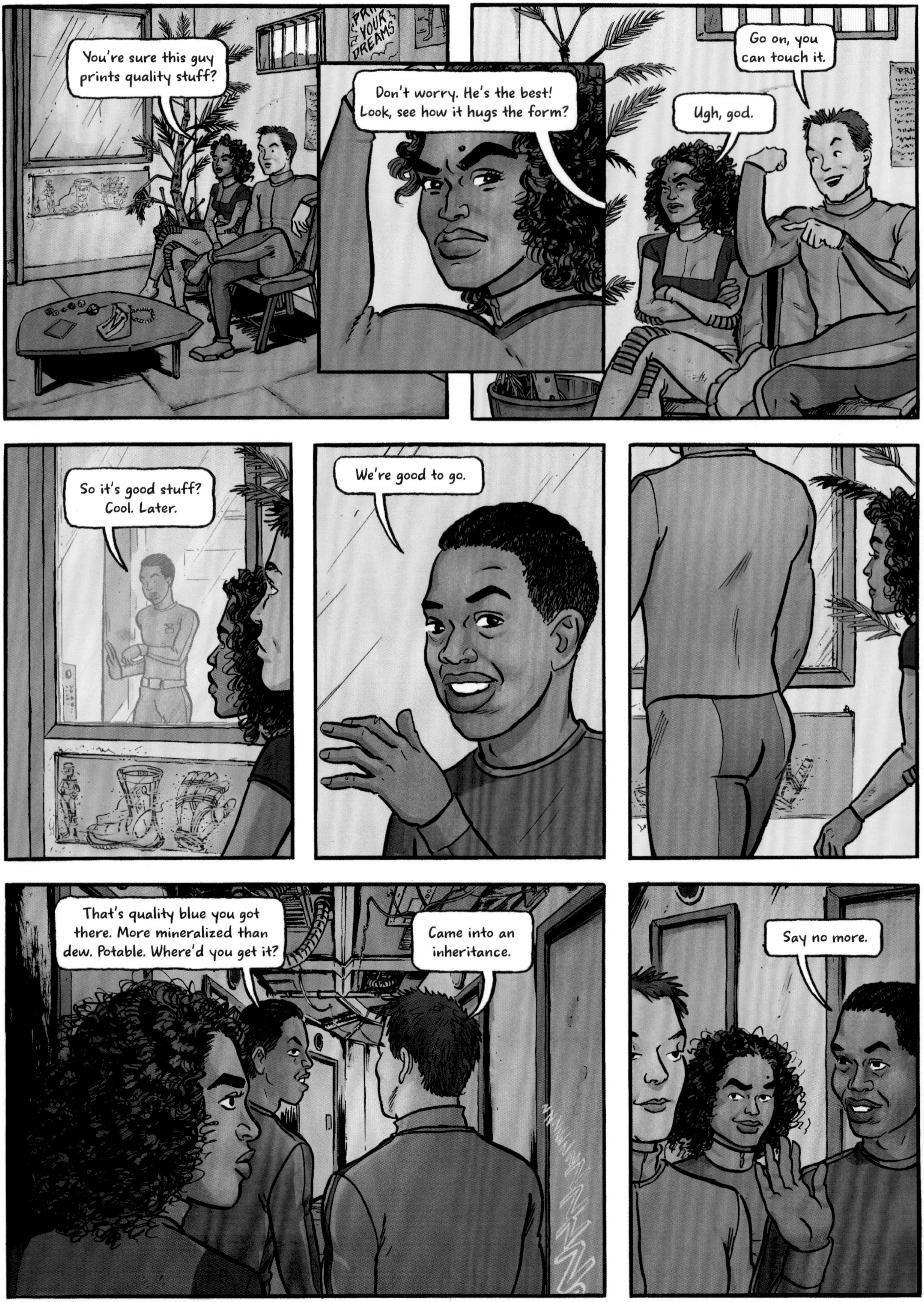
You're sure this guy prints quality stuff?
Don't worry. He's the best! Look, see how it hugs the form?
Go on, you can touch it.
Ugh, god.
So it's good stuff? Cool. Later.
We're good to go.
That's quality blue you got there. More mineralized than dew. Potable. Where'd you get it?
Came into an inheritance.
Say no more.

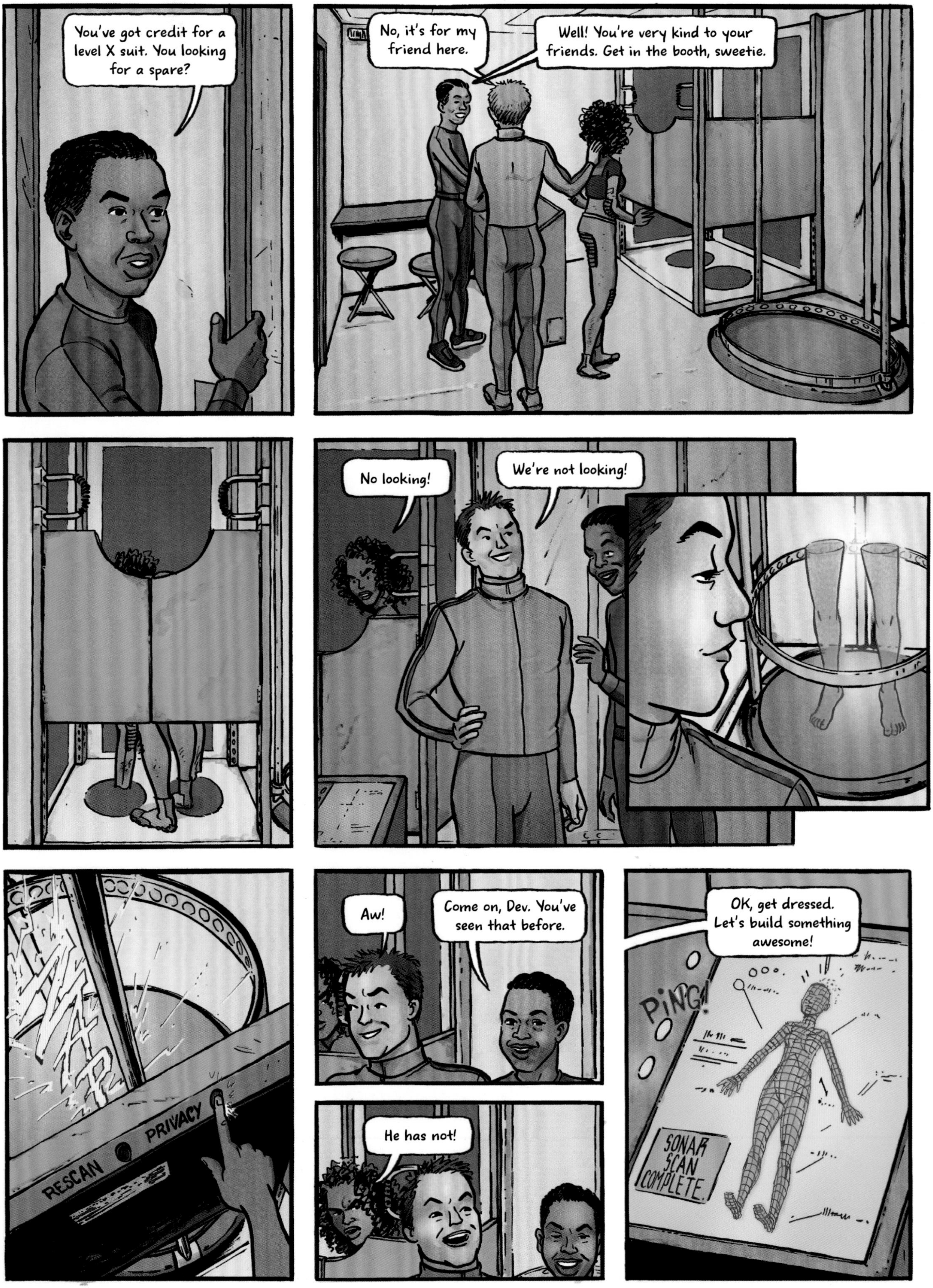
You've got credit for a level X suit. You looking for a spare?
No, it's for my friend here.
Well! You're very kind to your friends. Get in the booth, sweetie.
No looking!
We're not looking!
ZAP
PRIVACY
RESCAN
Aw!
Come on, Dev. You've seen that before.
He has not!
OK, get dressed. Let's build something awesome!
PING!
SONAR SCAN COMPLETE

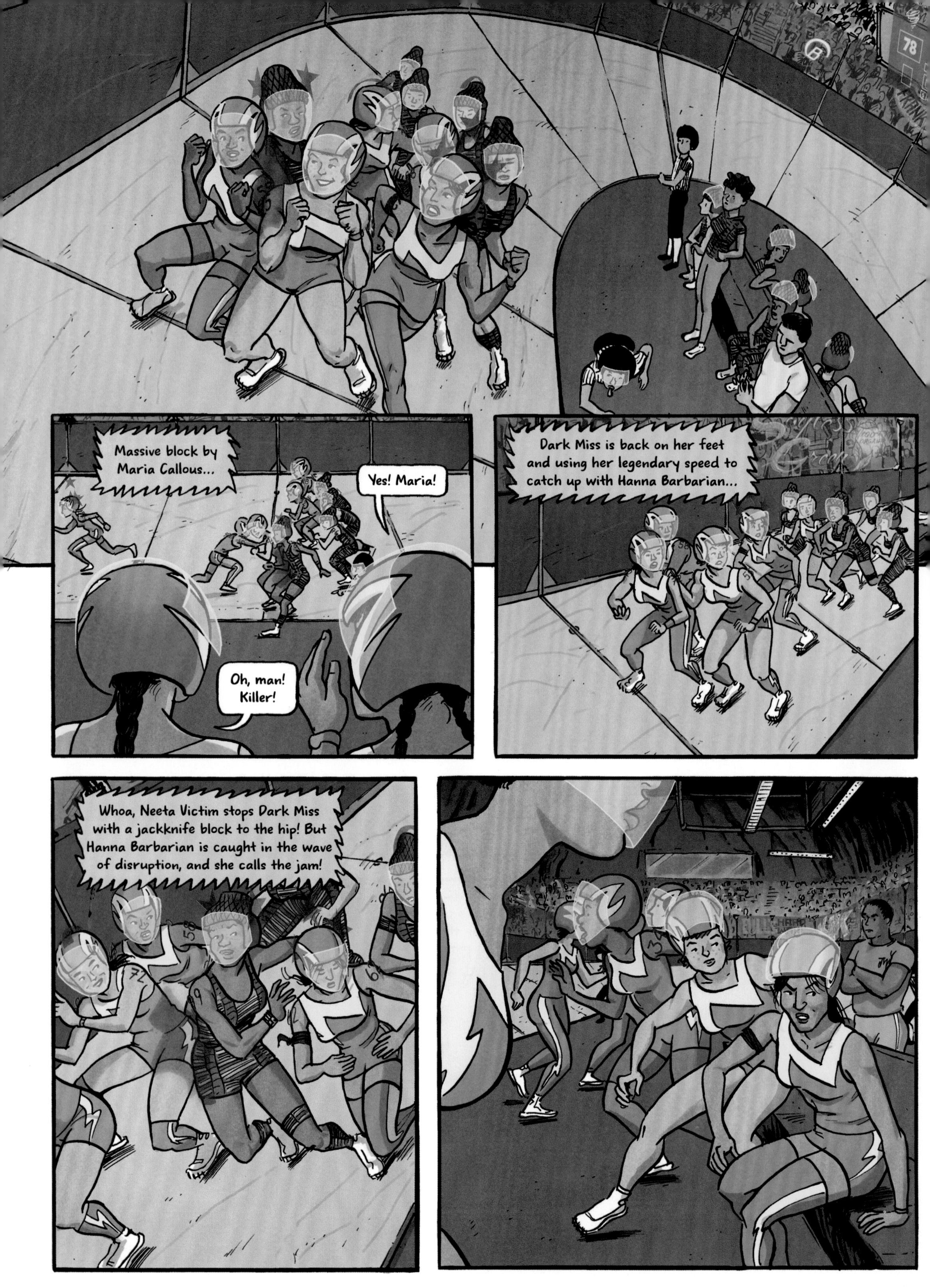

Massive block by Maria Callous...
Yes! Maria!
Oh, man! Killer!
Dark Miss is back on her feet and using her legendary speed to catch up with Hanna Barbarian...
Whoa, Neeta Victim stops Dark Miss with a jackknife block to the hip! But Hanna Barbarian is caught in the wave of disruption, and she calls the jam!

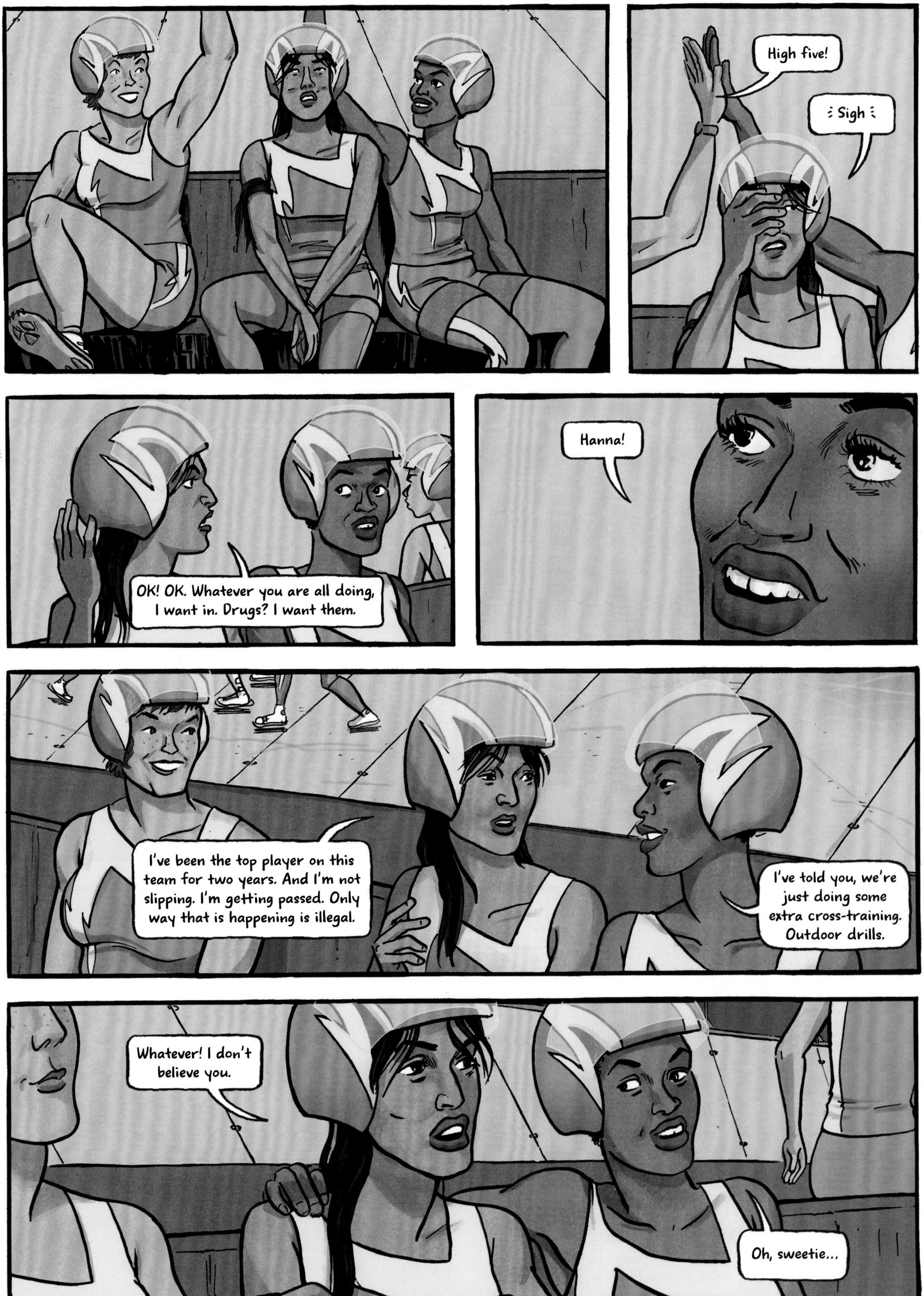
High five!
Sigh
OK! OK. Whatever you are all doing, I want in. Drugs? I want them.
Hanna!
I've been the top player on this team for two years. And I'm not slipping. I'm getting passed. Only way that is happening is illegal.
I've told you, we're just doing some extra cross-training. Outdoor drills.
Whatever! I don't believe you.
Oh, sweetie...

Don't "oh, sweetie" me.

Put me on the list. I plan to win the Derby Bowl this year.

Sure, Hanna. When we pass out the illegal performance-enhancing rocks, you're on the list.

You're so full of grot.

You're leaving in two days. Your little crew of supercharged players is getting smaller. Get me in.

We'll talk.

Right, Rocky? We'll talk.

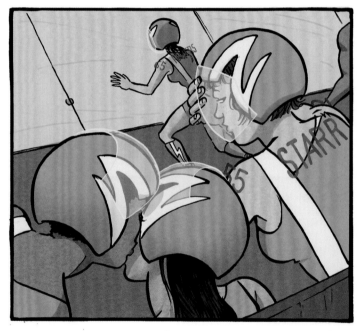

I can't believe you're with her.

Ha ha! Yeah, well. She's a handful.

With under two minutes on the clock, the Chaos leads at 92 to 89! This is a pivotal moment, folks.

Whoever wins today will play the Marineris Conference champion Minotaurs next week for a trip to the Derby Bowl!

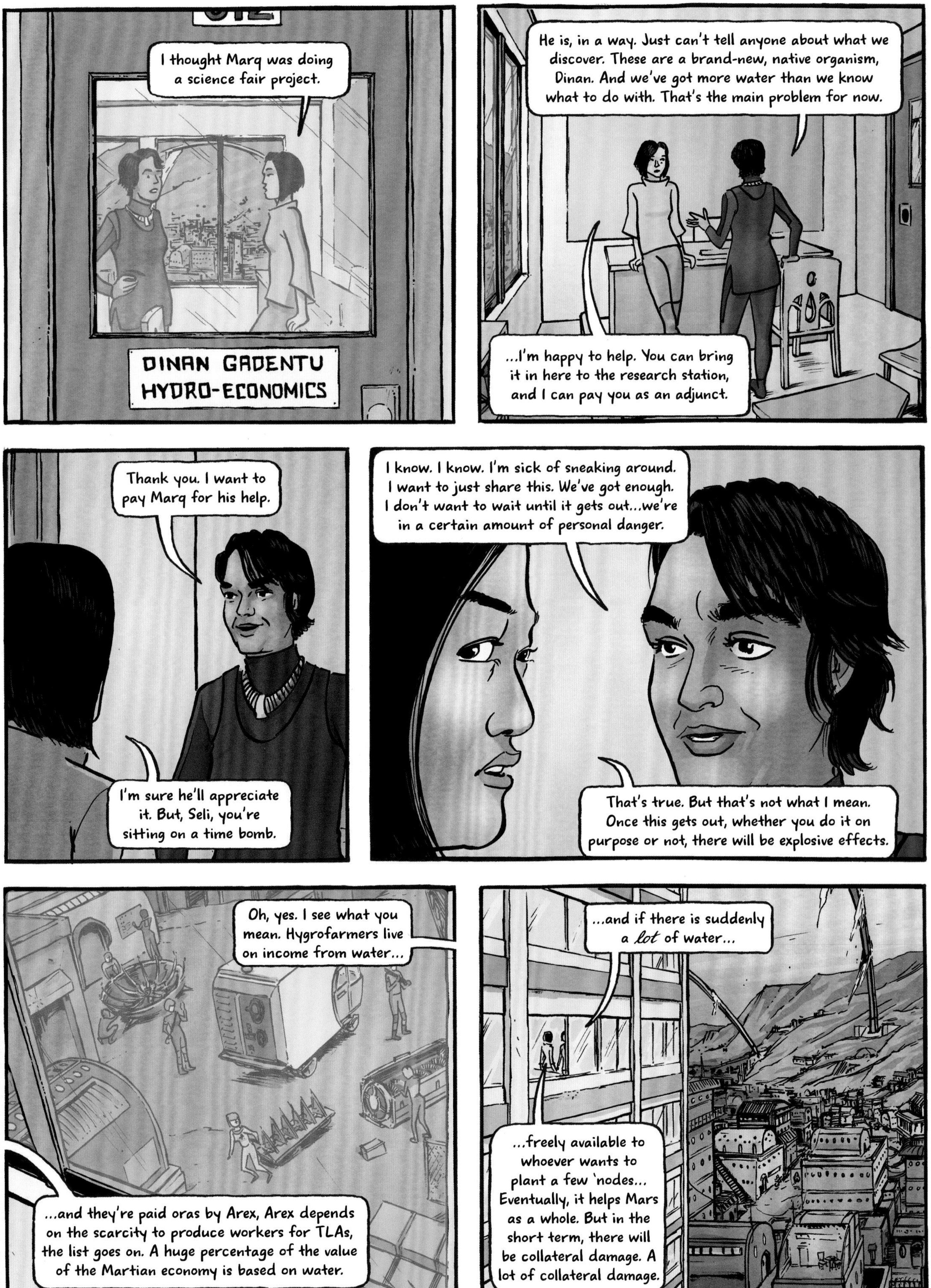

I thought Marq was doing a science fair project.
DINAN GADENTU
HYDRO-ECONOMICS
He is, in a way. Just can't tell anyone about what we discover. These are a brand-new, native organism, Dinan. And we've got more water than we know what to do with. That's the main problem for now.
...I'm happy to help. You can bring it in here to the research station, and I can pay you as an adjunct.
Thank you. I want to pay Marq for his help.
I'm sure he'll appreciate it. But, Seli, you're sitting on a time bomb.
I know. I know. I'm sick of sneaking around. I want to just share this. We've got enough. I don't want to wait until it gets out...we're in a certain amount of personal danger.
That's true. But that's not what I mean. Once this gets out, whether you do it on purpose or not, there will be explosive effects.
Oh, yes. I see what you mean. Hygrofarmers live on income from water...
...and they're paid oras by Arex, Arex depends on the scarcity to produce workers for TLAs, the list goes on. A huge percentage of the value of the Martian economy is based on water.
...and if there is suddenly a *lot* of water...
...freely available to whoever wants to plant a few 'nodes... Eventually, it helps Mars as a whole. But in the short term, there will be collateral damage. A lot of collateral damage.

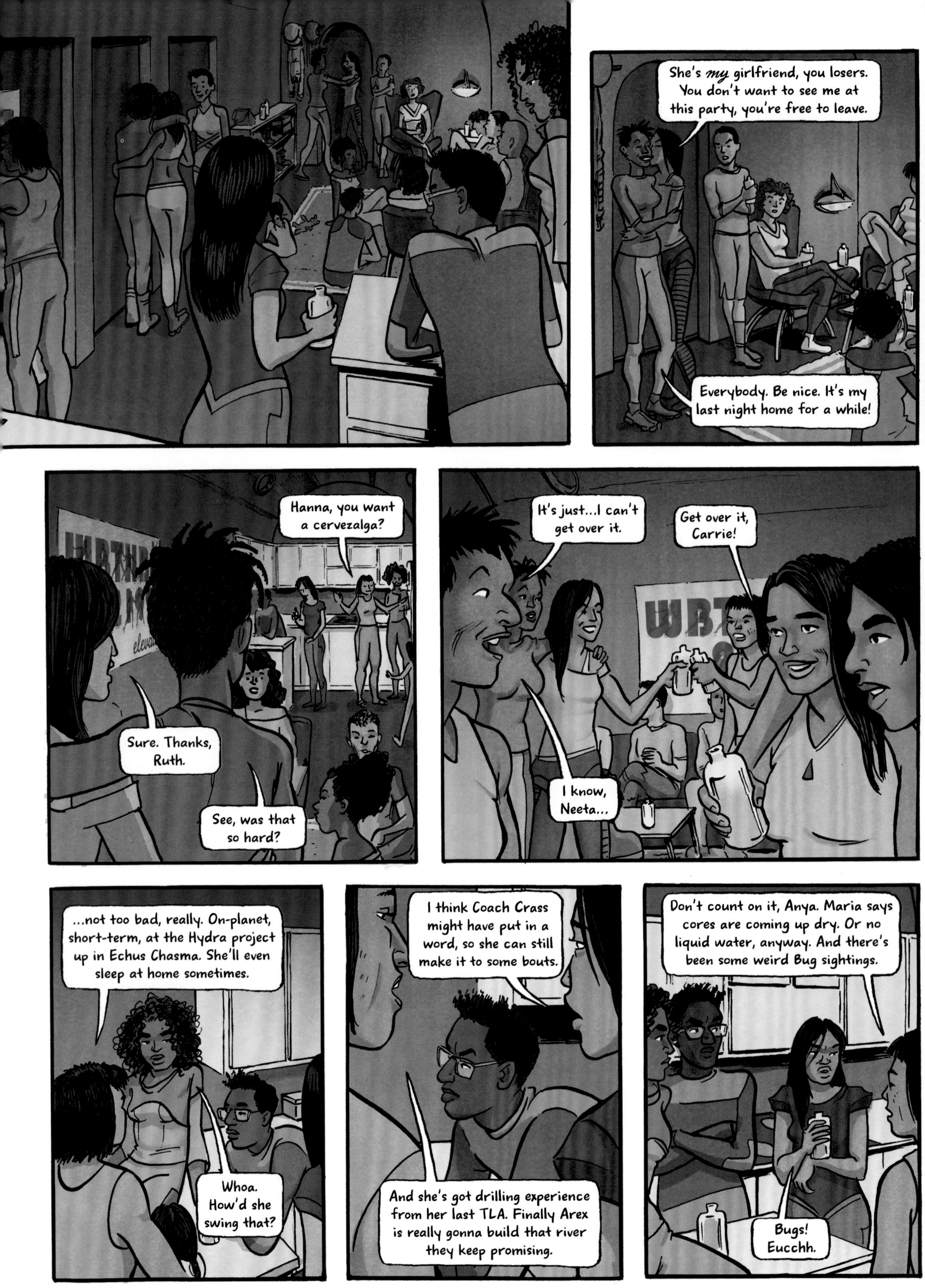
She's *my* girlfriend, you losers. You don't want to see me at this party, you're free to leave.
Everybody. Be nice. It's my last night home for a while!
Hanna, you want a cervezalga?
Sure. Thanks, Ruth.
See, was that so hard?
It's just...I can't get over it.
Get over it, Carrie!
I know, Neeta...
...not too bad, really. On-planet, short-term, at the Hydra project up in Echus Chasma. She'll even sleep at home sometimes.
Whoa. How'd she swing that?
I think Coach Crass might have put in a word, so she can still make it to some bouts.
And she's got drilling experience from her last TLA. Finally Arex is really gonna build that river they keep promising.
Don't count on it, Anya. Maria says cores are coming up dry. Or no liquid water, anyway. And there's been some weird Bug sightings.
Bugs! Eucchh.

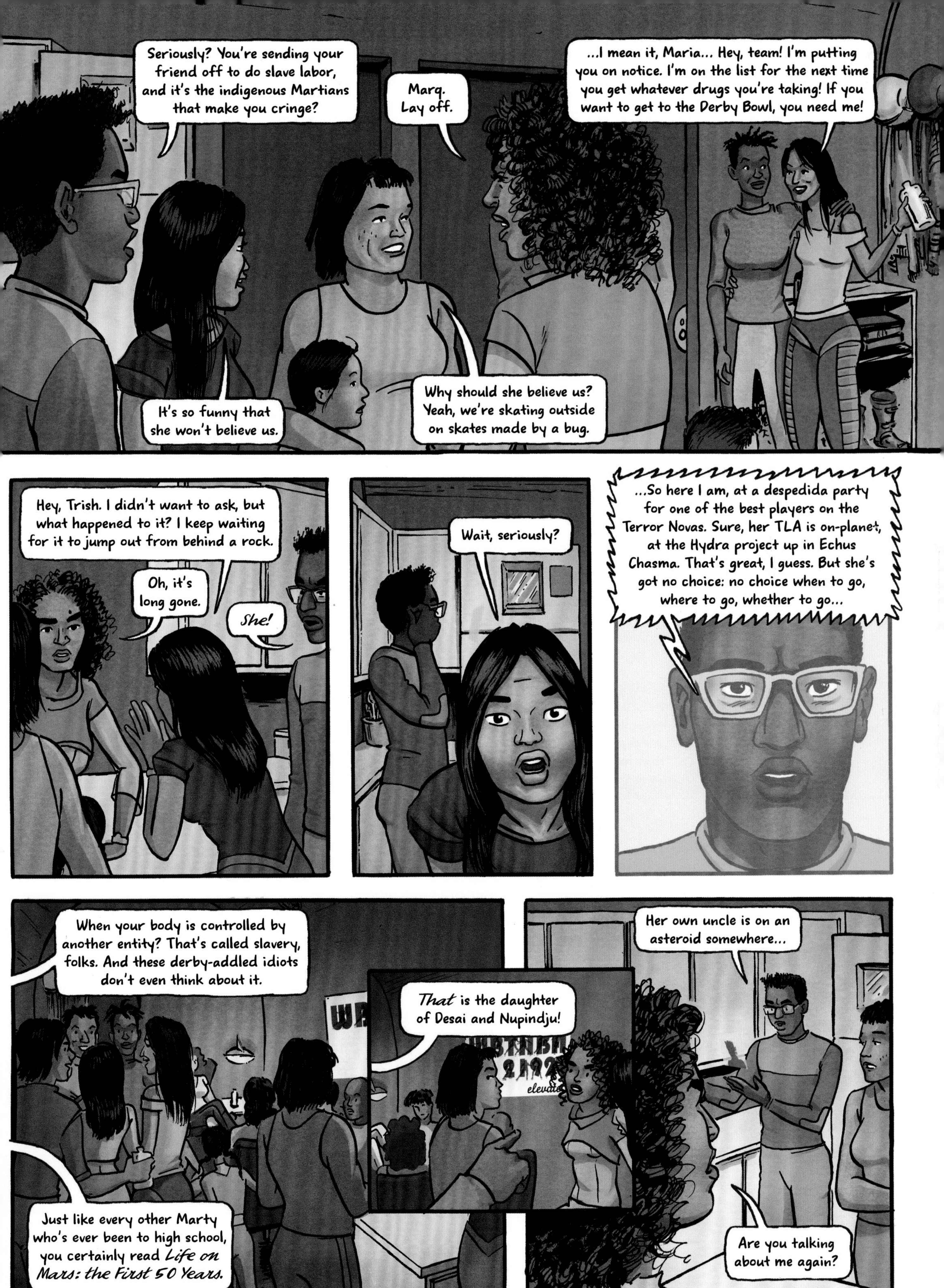
Seriously? You're sending your friend off to do slave labor, and it's the indigenous Martians that make you cringe?
Marq. Lay off.
...I mean it, Maria... Hey, team! I'm putting you on notice. I'm on the list for the next time you get whatever drugs you're taking! If you want to get to the Derby Bowl, you need me!
It's so funny that she won't believe us.
Why should she believe us? Yeah, we're skating outside on skates made by a bug.
Hey, Trish. I didn't want to ask, but what happened to it? I keep waiting for it to jump out from behind a rock.
Oh, it's long gone.
She!
Wait, seriously?
...So here I am, at a despedida party for one of the best players on the Terror Novas. Sure, her TLA is on-planet, at the Hydra project up in Echus Chasma. That's great, I guess. But she's got no choice: no choice when to go, where to go, whether to go...
When your body is controlled by another entity? That's called slavery, folks. And these derby-addled idiots don't even think about it.
Just like every other Marty who's ever been to high school, you certainly read *Life on Mars: the First 50 Years.*
That is the daughter of Desai and Nupindju!
Her own uncle is on an asteroid somewhere...
Are you talking about me again?

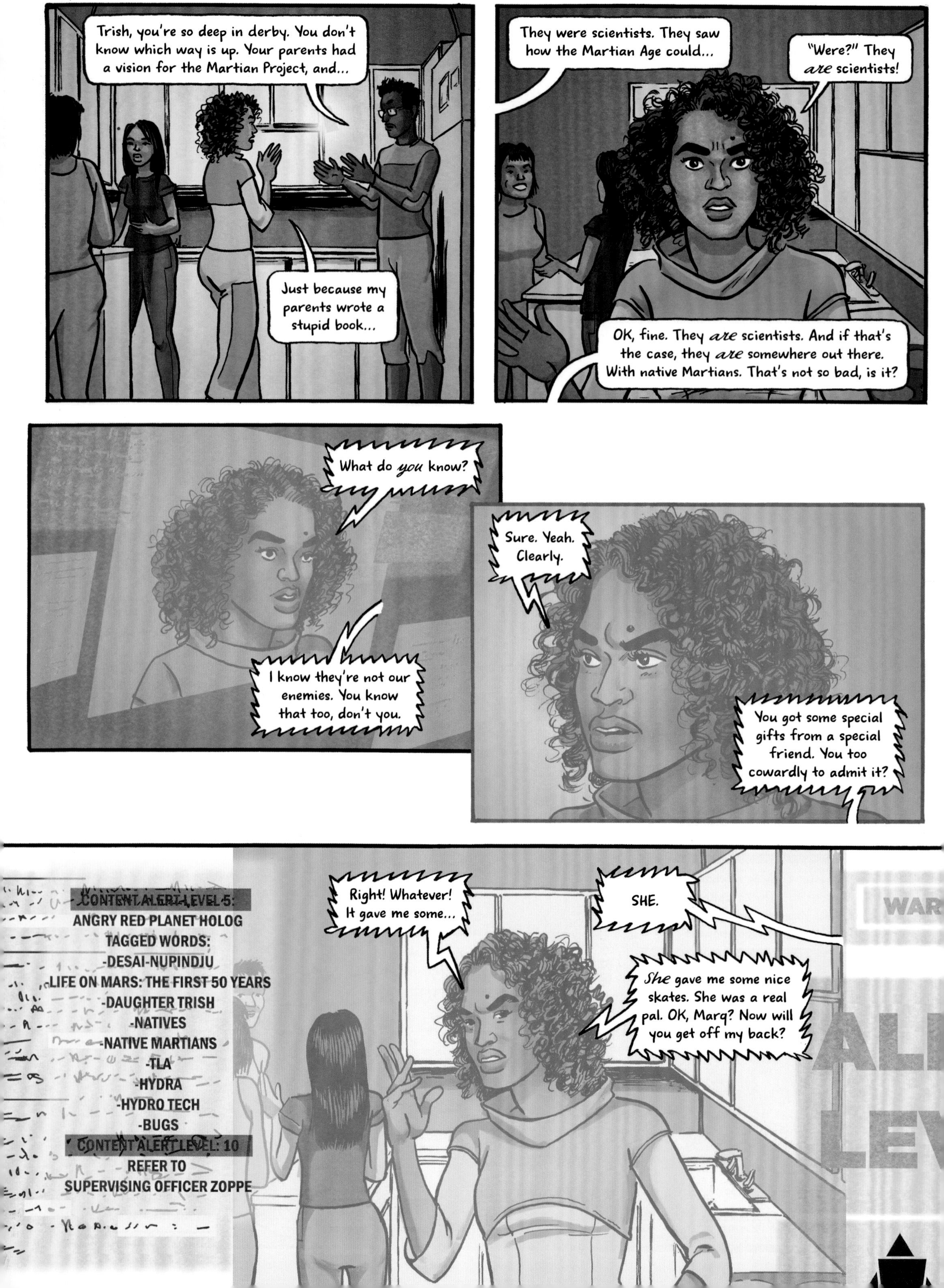
Trish, you're so deep in derby. You don't know which way is up. Your parents had a vision for the Martian Project, and...
Just because my parents wrote a stupid book...
They were scientists. They saw how the Martian Age could...
"Were?" They *are* scientists!
OK, fine. They *are* scientists. And if that's the case, they *are* somewhere out there. With native Martians. That's not so bad, is it?
What do *you* know?
I know they're not our enemies. You know that too, don't you.
Sure. Yeah. Clearly.
You got some special gifts from a special friend. You too cowardly to admit it?
CONTENT ALERT LEVEL 5:
ANGRY RED PLANET HOLOG
TAGGED WORDS:
-DESAI-NUPINDJU
-LIFE ON MARS: THE FIRST 50 YEARS
-DAUGHTER TRISH
-NATIVES
-NATIVE MARTIANS
-TLA
-HYDRA
-HYDRO TECH
-BUGS
CONTENT ALERT LEVEL: 10
REFER TO
SUPERVISING OFFICER ZOPPE
Right! Whatever! It gave me some...
SHE.
She gave me some nice skates. She was a real pal. OK, Marq? Now will you get off my back?

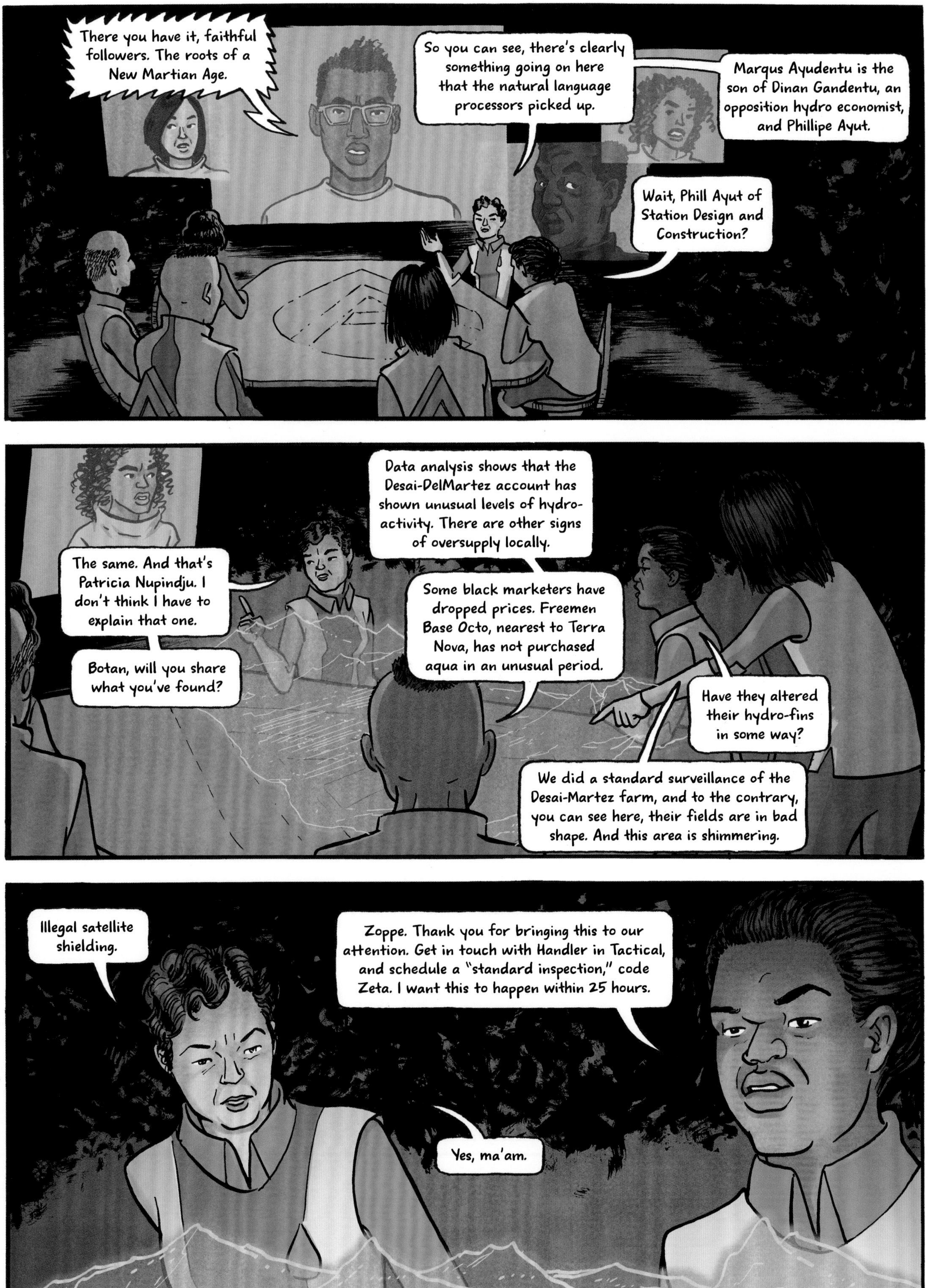

There you have it, faithful followers. The roots of a New Martian Age.
So you can see, there's clearly something going on here that the natural language processors picked up.
Marqus Ayudentu is the son of Dinan Gandentu, an opposition hydro economist, and Phillipe Ayut.
Wait, Phill Ayut of Station Design and Construction?
The same. And that's Patricia Nupindju. I don't think I have to explain that one.
Botan, will you share what you've found?
Data analysis shows that the Desai-DelMartez account has shown unusual levels of hydro-activity. There are other signs of oversupply locally.
Some black marketers have dropped prices. Freemen Base Octo, nearest to Terra Nova, has not purchased aqua in an unusual period.
Have they altered their hydro-fins in some way?
We did a standard surveillance of the Desai-Martez farm, and to the contrary, you can see here, their fields are in bad shape. And this area is shimmering.
Illegal satellite shielding.
Zoppe. Thank you for bringing this to our attention. Get in touch with Handler in Tactical, and schedule a "standard inspection," code Zeta. I want this to happen within 25 hours.
Yes, ma'am.

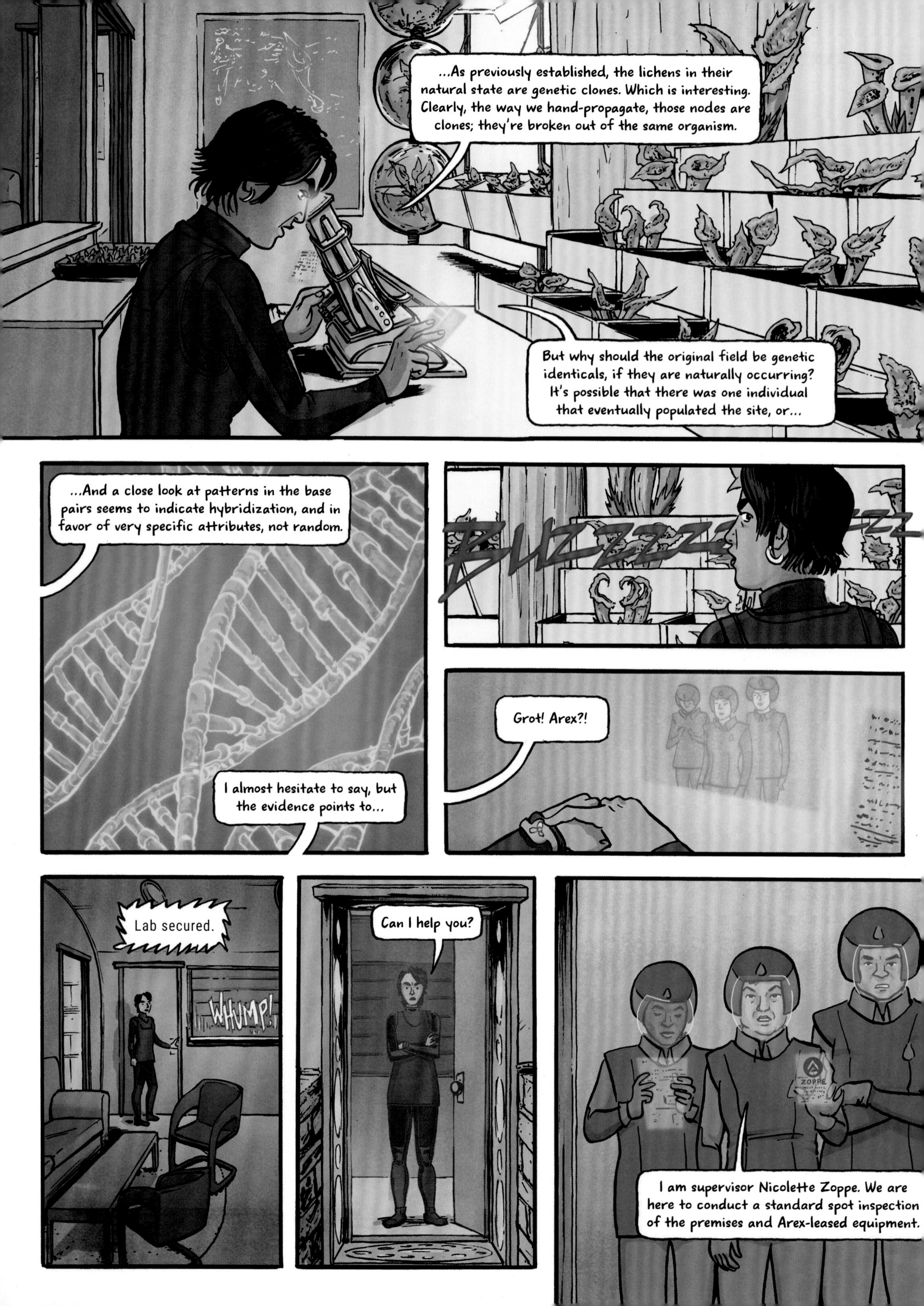

...As previously established, the lichens in their natural state are genetic clones. Which is interesting. Clearly, the way we hand-propagate, those nodes are clones; they're broken out of the same organism.
But why should the original field be genetic identicals, if they are naturally occurring? It's possible that there was one individual that eventually populated the site, or...
...And a close look at patterns in the base pairs seems to indicate hybridization, and in favor of very specific attributes, not random.
I almost hesitate to say, but the evidence points to...
BUZZZZZ
Grot! Arex?!
Lab secured.
WHUMP!
Can I help you?
I am supervisor Nicolette Zoppe. We are here to conduct a standard spot inspection of the premises and Arex-leased equipment.

2.76 millimeters.

That will entail a fine of...1267.79 oras.

Ms. Desai, you are not exhibiting a proper level of dust management awareness. This is rather shocking...

It's a grotting dust bowl out here!

You're not tanking H₂O, your place has practically gone back to regolith: are you *trying* to catch a TLA? Where's your thresher? Our thresher, I should say.

What my colleague means to say is, we're here to help you upgrade your dust-management procedure.

I don't need help.

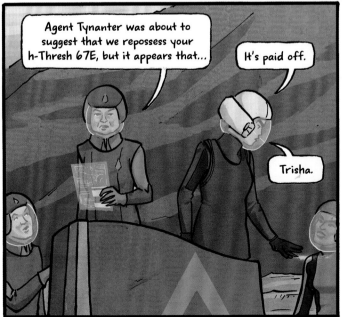

Agent Tynanter was about to suggest that we repossess your h-Thresh 67E, but it appears that...

It's paid off.

Trisha.

Right, well. And your house. Paid off. Recently, it seems.

I've been consulting for the college. I haven't had time to clean my fields.

Ms. Desai, we colonists—Martys—we depend on you moisture farmers for our most precious resource!

We simply can't have you frittering away the resources we've invested in...

Listen, you Duster. We don't care if you're busy. You may own that shed, but this installation is property of Arex, and we expect it to be maintained...and used.

I'm afraid there's an additional issue. Our bots have identified an area of your Homestead that is under satellite shielding. I must remind you, Homestead Allotments are not permitted to be shielded until fully vested.

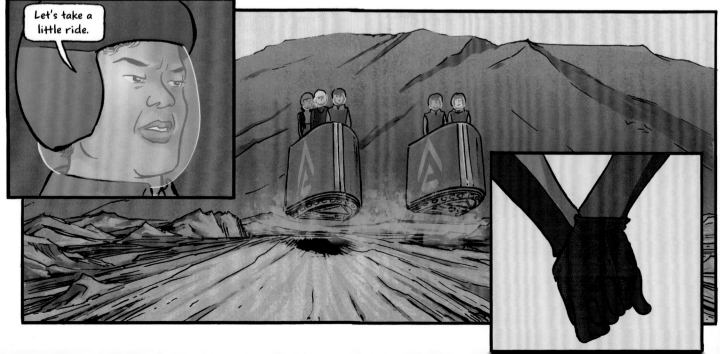

Let's take a little ride.

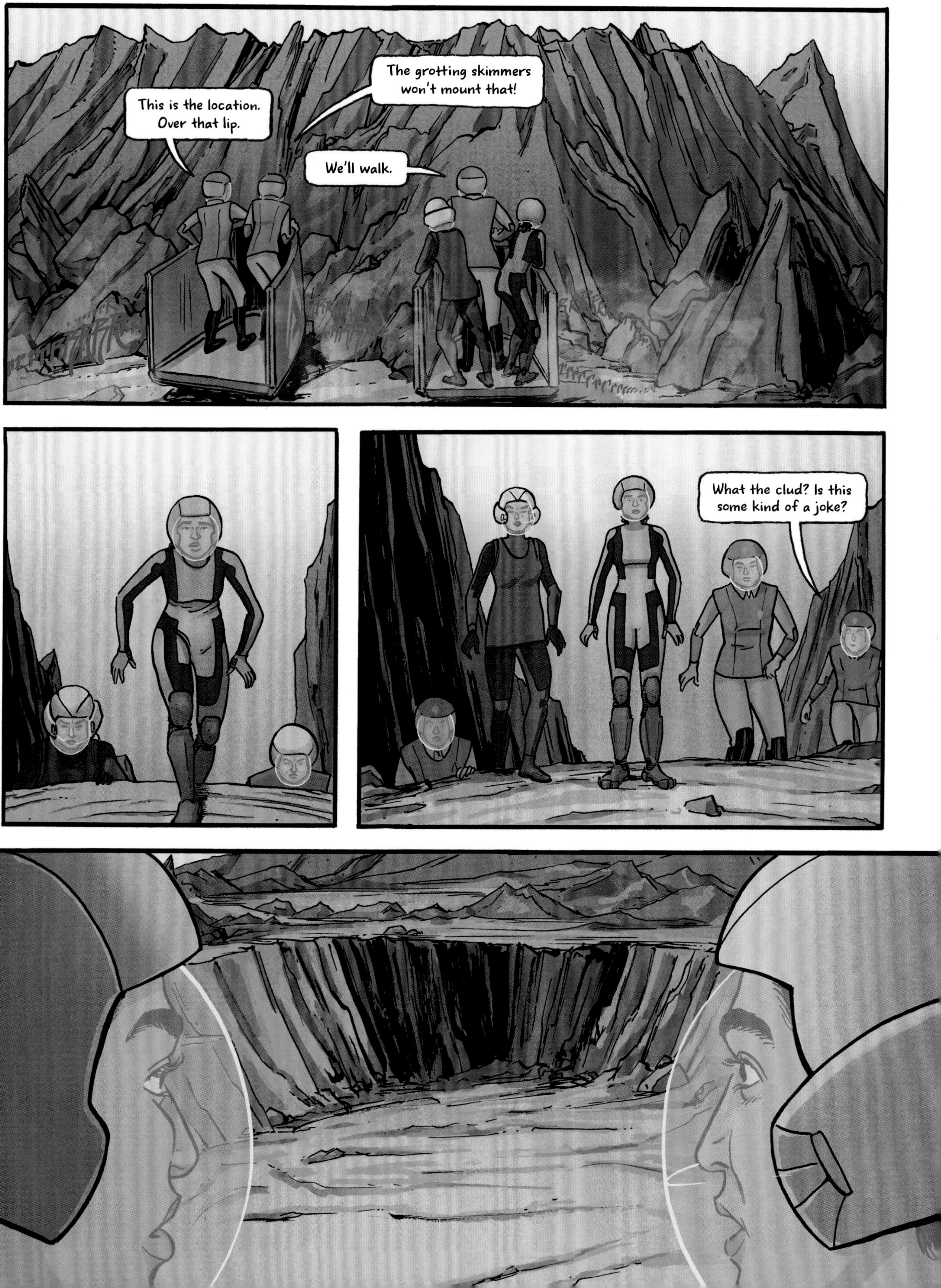
This is the location. Over that lip.
The grotting skimmers won't mount that!
We'll walk.
What the clud? Is this some kind of a joke?

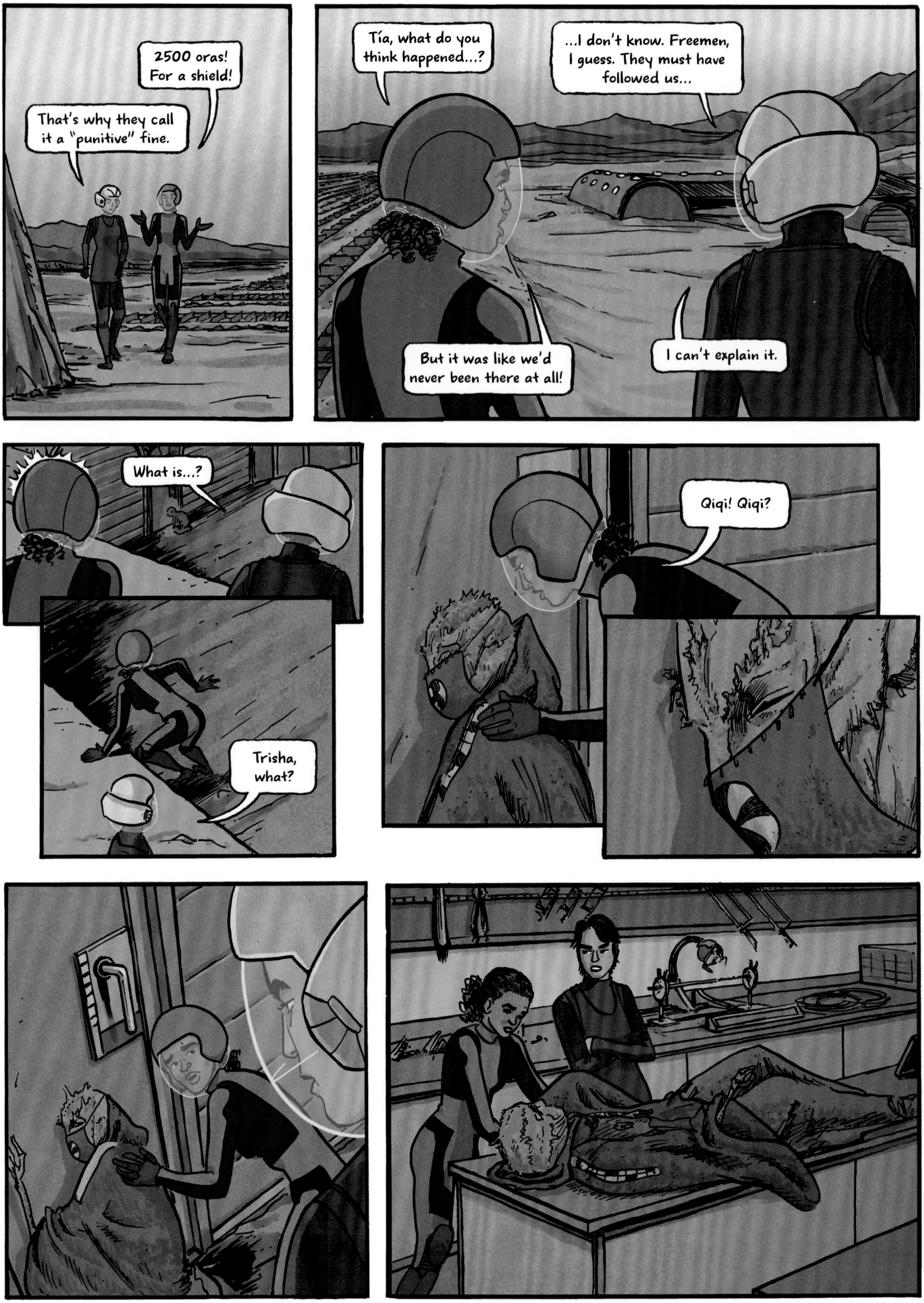
2500 oras! For a shield!
That's why they call it a "punitive" fine.
Tía, what do you think happened...?
...I don't know. Freemen, I guess. They must have followed us...
But it was like we'd never been there at all!
I can't explain it.
What is...?
Trisha, what?
Qiqi! Qiqi?

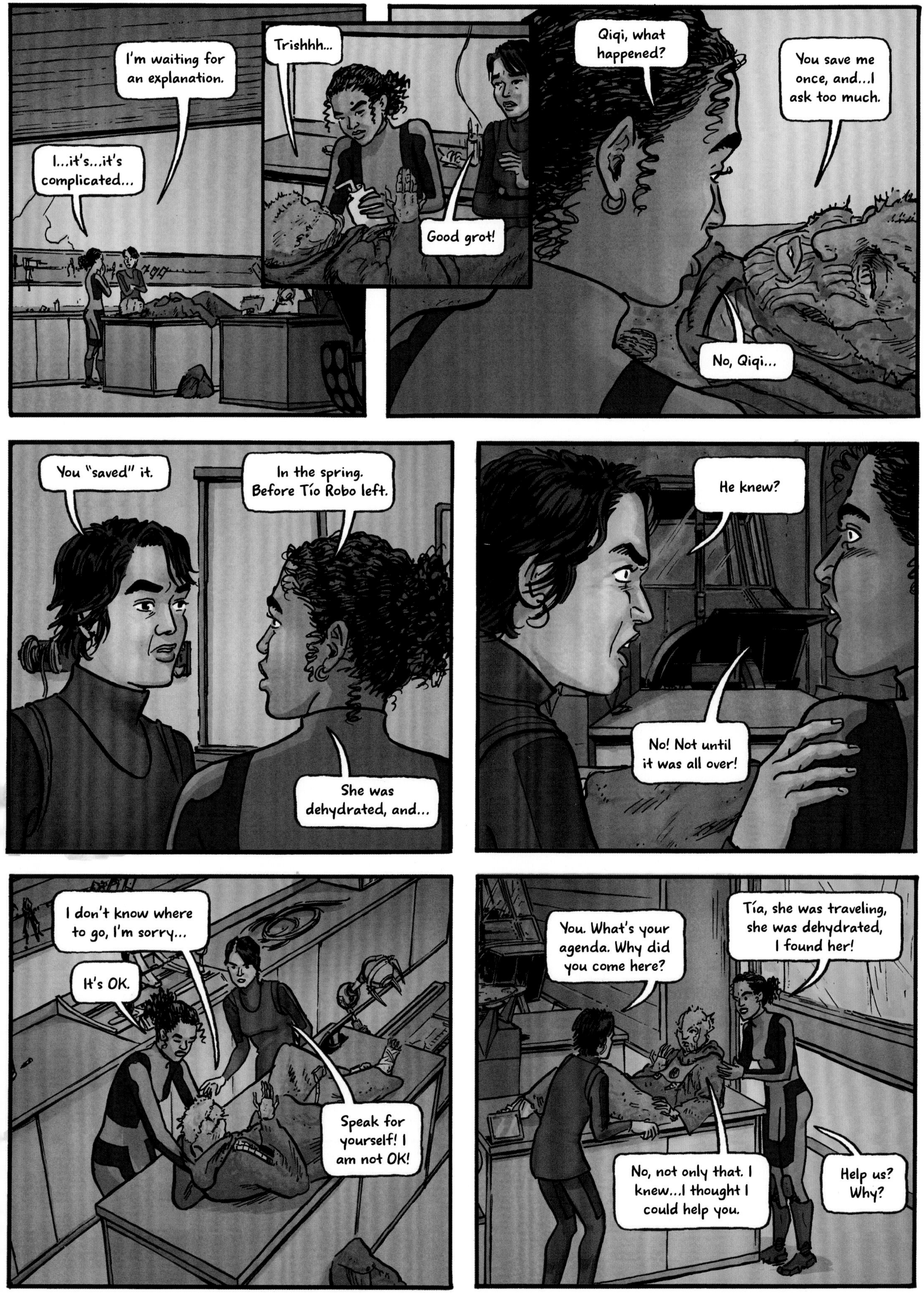
I'm waiting for an explanation.
I...it's...it's complicated...
Trishhh...
Good grot!
Qiqi, what happened?
You save me once, and...I ask too much.
No, Qiqi...
You "saved" it.
In the spring. Before Tío Robo left.
She was dehydrated, and...
He knew?
No! Not until it was all over!
I don't know where to go, I'm sorry...
It's OK.
Speak for yourself! I am not OK!
You. What's your agenda. Why did you come here?
Tía, she was traveling, she was dehydrated, I found her!
No, not only that. I knew...I thought I could help you.
Help us? Why?

I wanted to tell you but it wasn't safe. I bring lich'khens because I know you need water. I know from...

You brought the... that explains their hybridized DNA...

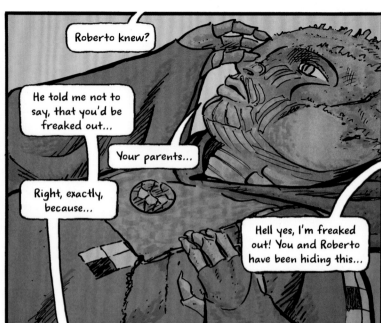

Roberto knew?

He told me not to say, that you'd be freaked out...

Your parents...

Right, exactly, because...

Hell yes, I'm freaked out! You and Roberto have been hiding this...

Now my people cast me out. They discover that I give lich-khen. They say I am malformed.

Wait, what?

I am...not like-kt them. No one tells me to do, I *decide* for me. I have...ideazz. I am born wrong.

Your people don't make decisions?

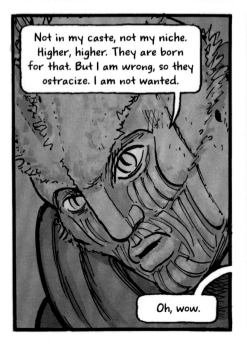

Not in my caste, not my niche. Higher, higher. They are born for that. But I am wrong, so they ostracize. I am not wanted.

Oh, wow.

...And now, I do not-tk know where to go. My clan drop me here, take lich-khen from field...

Take lichen? You mean they took the nodes?

They clean the land.

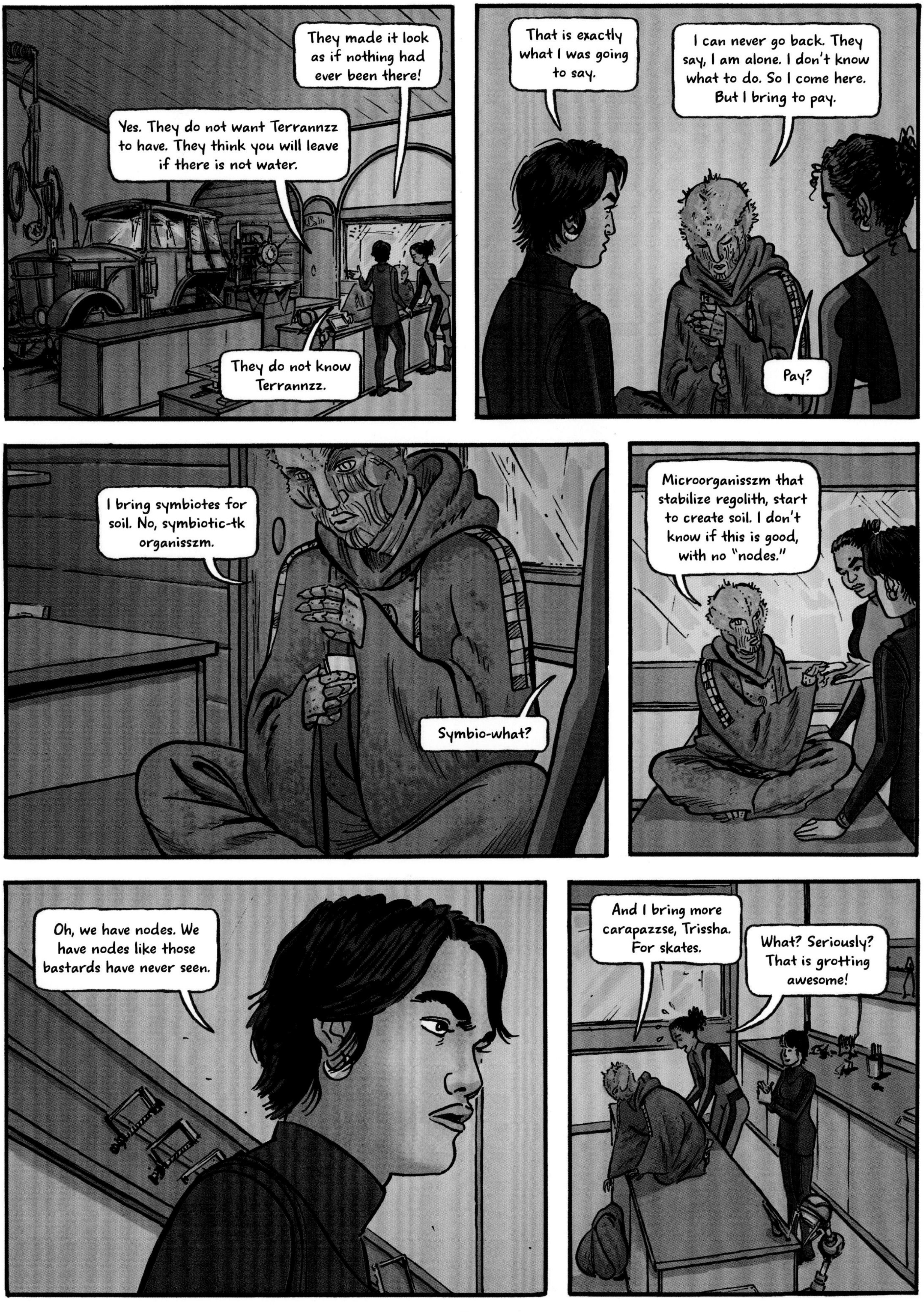
They made it look as if nothing had ever been there!
Yes. They do not want Terrannzz to have. They think you will leave if there is not water.
They do not know Terrannzz.
That is exactly what I was going to say.
I can never go back. They say, I am alone. I don't know what to do. So I come here. But I bring to pay.
Pay?
I bring symbiotes for soil. No, symbiotic-tk organisszm.
Symbio-what?
Microorganisszm that stabilize regolith, start to create soil. I don't know if this is good, with no "nodes."
Oh, we have nodes. We have nodes like those bastards have never seen.
And I bring more carapazzse, Trissha. For skates.
What? Seriously? That is grotting awesome!

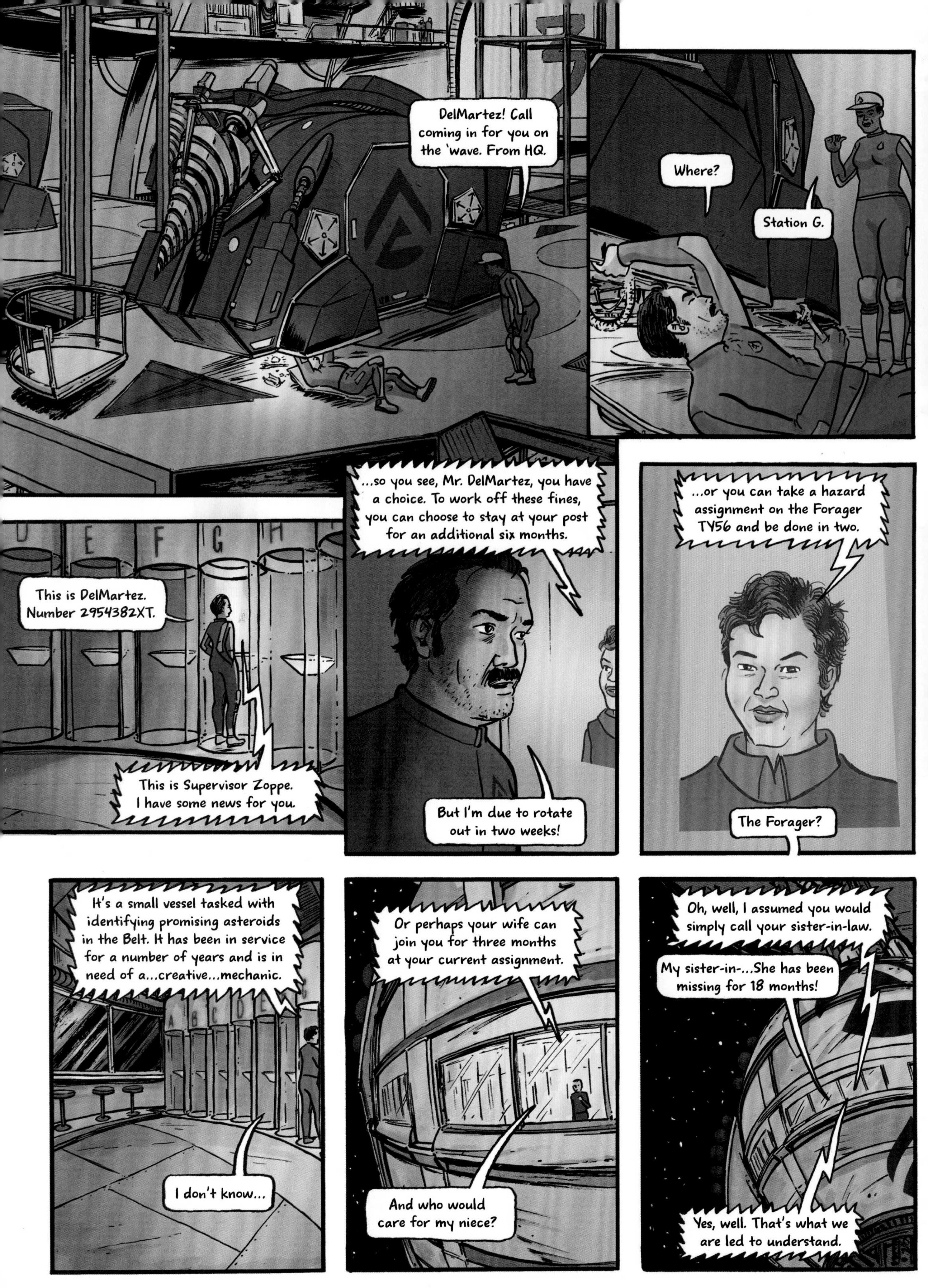
DelMartez! Call coming in for you on the 'wave. From HQ.
Where?
Station G.
This is DelMartez. Number 2954382XT.
This is Supervisor Zoppe. I have some news for you.
...so you see, Mr. DelMartez, you have a choice. To work off these fines, you can choose to stay at your post for an additional six months.
But I'm due to rotate out in two weeks!
...or you can take a hazard assignment on the Forager TY56 and be done in two.
The Forager?
It's a small vessel tasked with identifying promising asteroids in the Belt. It has been in service for a number of years and is in need of a...creative...mechanic.
I don't know...
Or perhaps your wife can join you for three months at your current assignment.
And who would care for my niece?
Oh, well, I assumed you would simply call your sister-in-law.
My sister-in-...She has been missing for 18 months!
Yes, well. That's what we are led to understand.

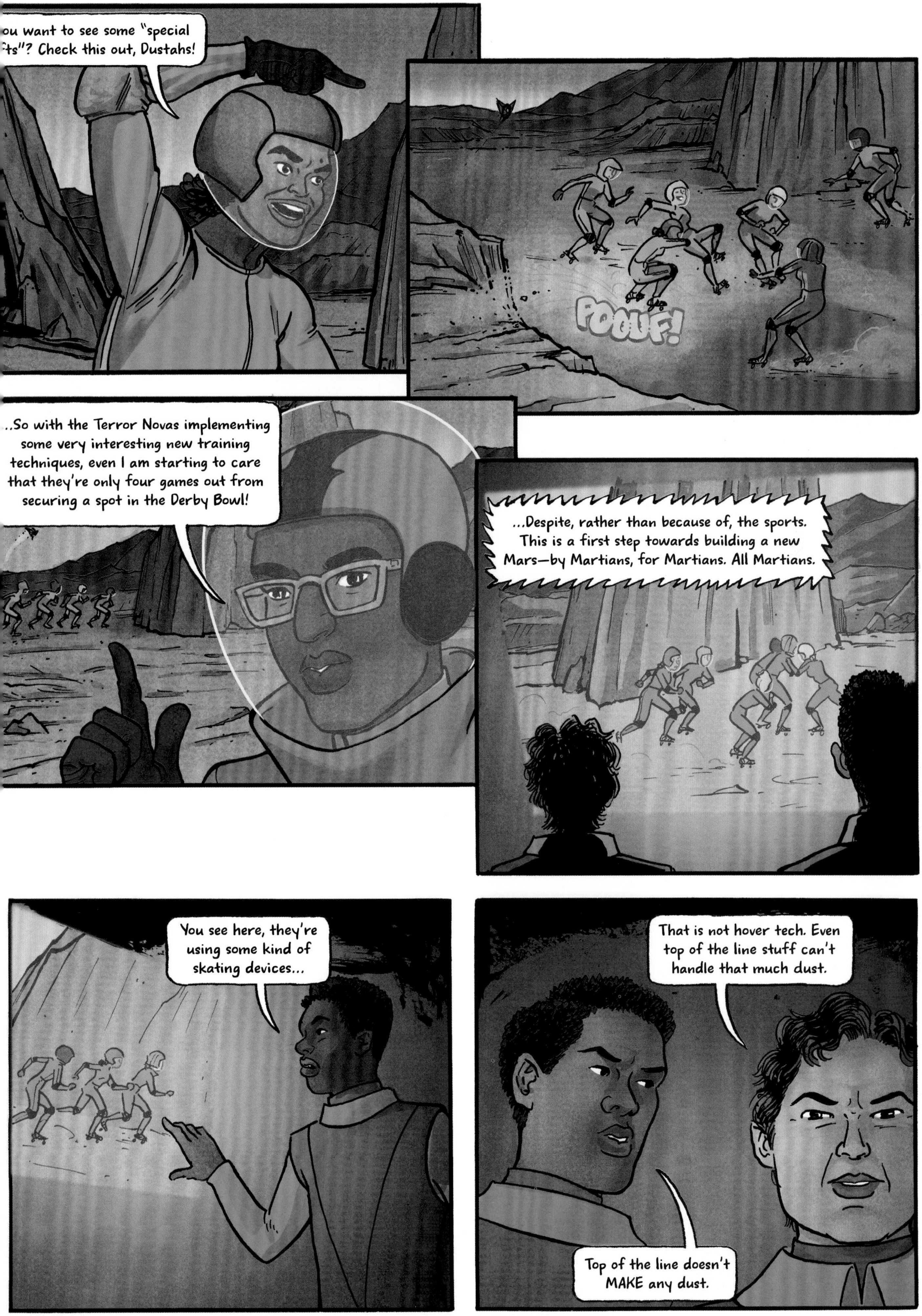
ou want to see some "special
-ts"? Check this out, Dustahs!
POOUF!
...So with the Terror Novas implementing some very interesting new training techniques, even I am starting to care that they're only four games out from securing a spot in the Derby Bowl!
...Despite, rather than because of, the sports. This is a first step towards building a new Mars—by Martians, for Martians. All Martians.
You see here, they're using some kind of skating devices...
That is not hover tech. Even top of the line stuff can't handle that much dust.
Top of the line doesn't MAKE any dust.

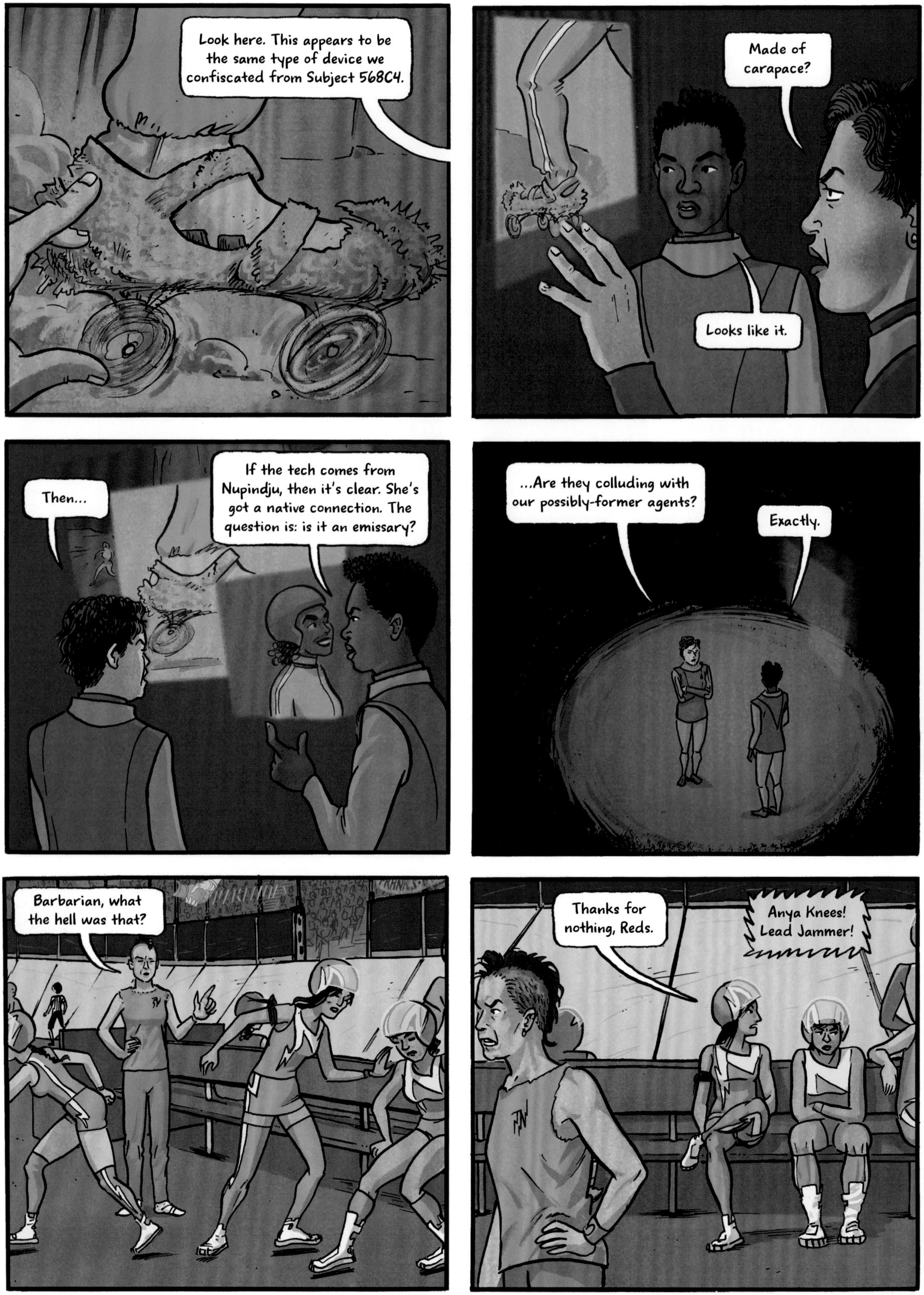
Look here. This appears to be the same type of device we confiscated from Subject 568C4.
Made of carapace?
Looks like it.
Then...
If the tech comes from Nupindju, then it's clear. She's got a native connection. The question is: is it an emissary?
...Are they colluding with our possibly-former agents?
Exactly.
Barbarian, what the hell was that?
Thanks for nothing, Reds.
Anya Knees! Lead Jammer!

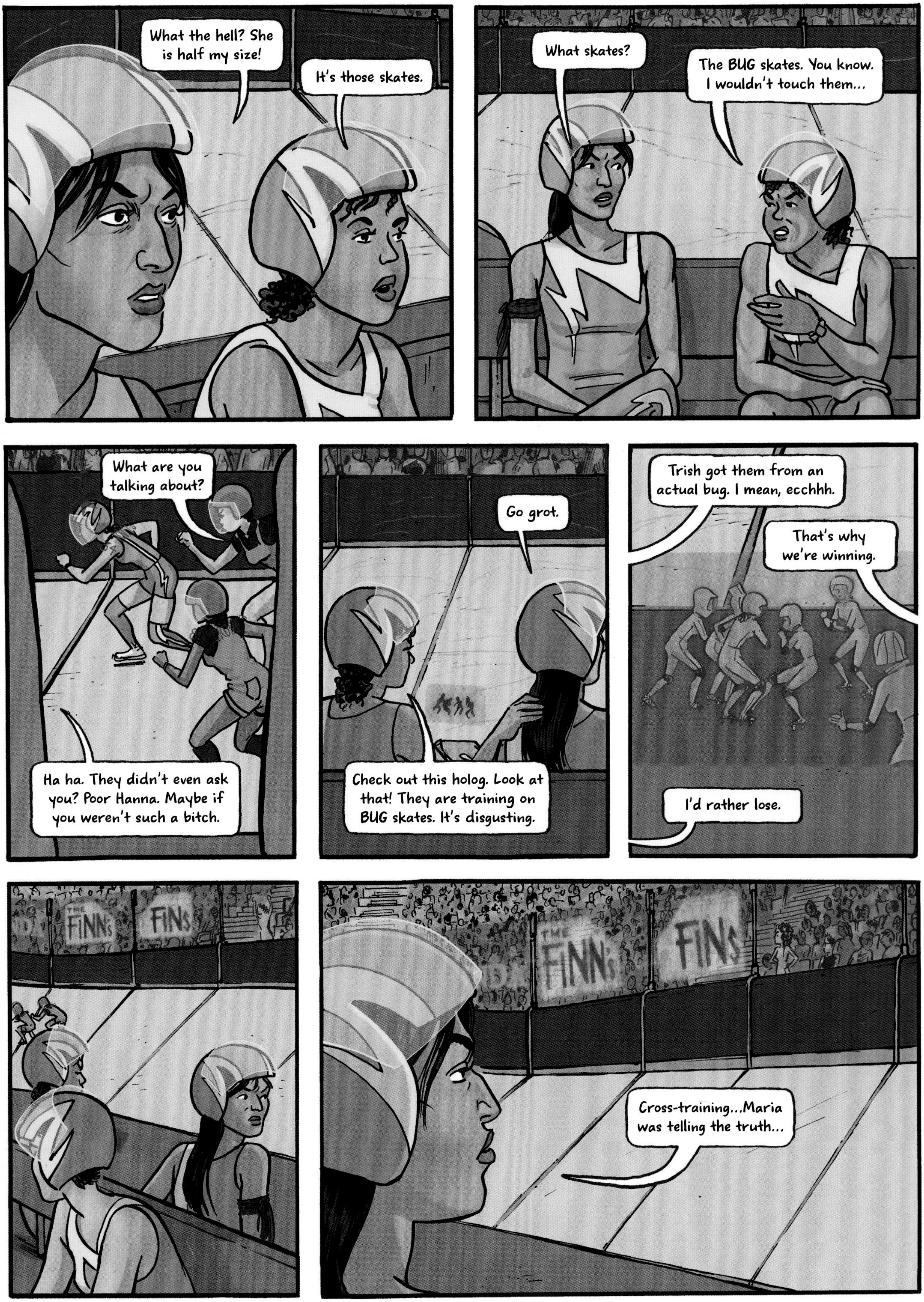
What the hell? She is half my size!
It's those skates.
What skates?
The BUG skates. You know. I wouldn't touch them...
What are you talking about?
Ha ha. They didn't even ask you? Poor Hanna. Maybe if you weren't such a bitch.
Go grot.
Check out this holog. Look at that! They are training on BUG skates. It's disgusting.
Trish got them from an actual bug. I mean, ecchhh.
That's why we're winning.
I'd rather lose.
THE FINN's
FINs
THE FINN's
FINs
Cross-training...Maria was telling the truth...

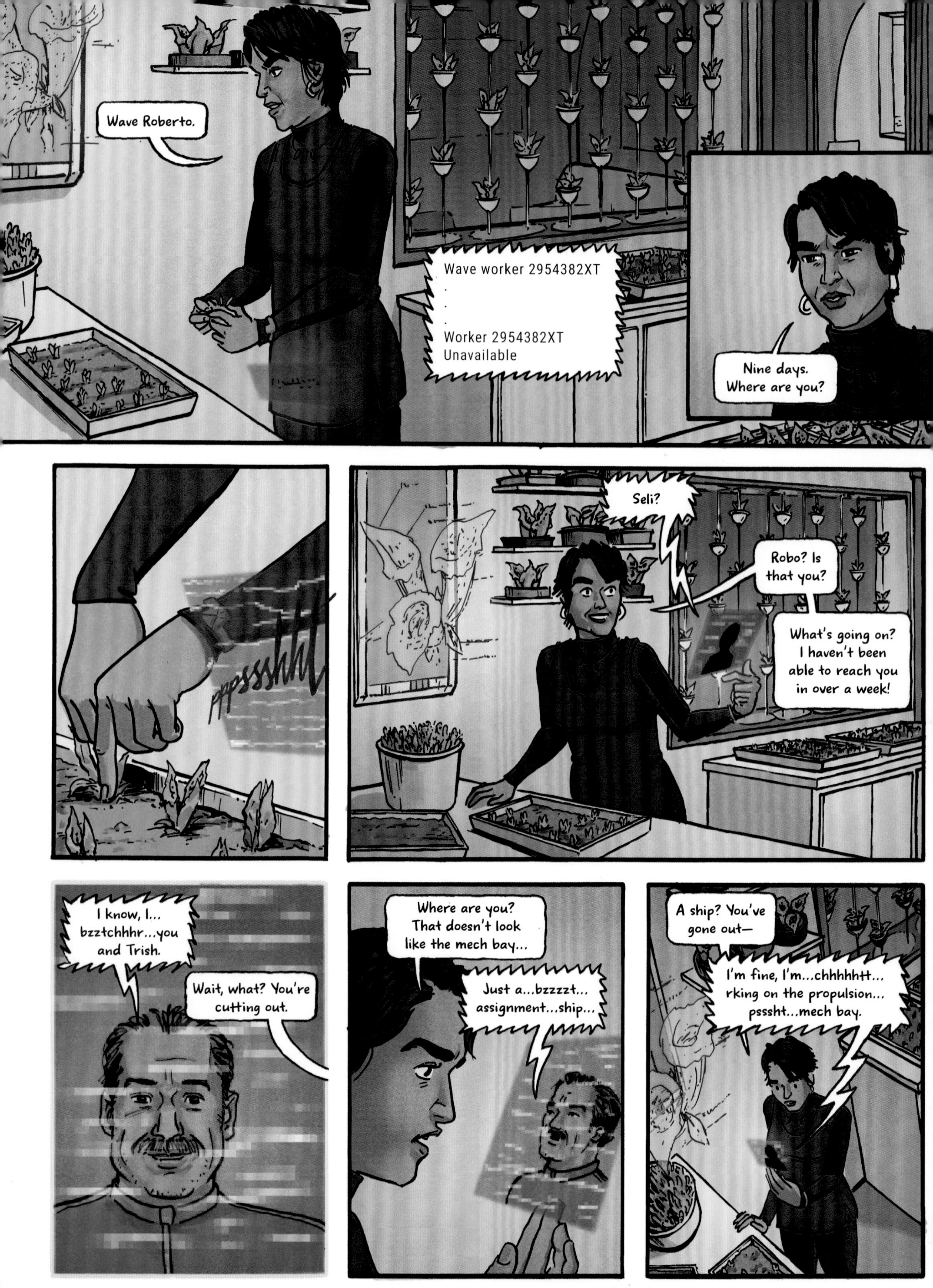
Wave Roberto.
Wave worker 2954382XT
.
.
.
Worker 2954382XT
Unavailable
Nine days. Where are you?
pppssshhh
Seli?
Robo? Is that you?
What's going on? I haven't been able to reach you in over a week!
I know, I... bzztchhhr...you and Trish.
Wait, what? You're cutting out.
Where are you? That doesn't look like the mech bay...
Just a...bzzzzt... assignment...ship...
A ship? You've gone out—
I'm fine, I'm...chhhhhtt... rking on the propulsion... psssht...mech bay.

You're in the mech bay? Roberto—

...short assign...chhhrrrr... per Belt...chhhht...diation interference...

Are you all right? You look thin.

pssssht...nnection. I'll call soon. I love you... tsshhht...Trish.

Robo, wait, don't hang up! Wait! I love you!

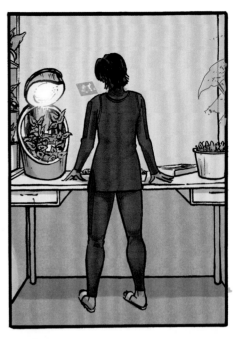

BUZZZZT

Not again!

Trish! You've got a friend at the front door!

What?

Hanna? But the living room is full of nodes!

Bring her around to the garage.

But, Qiqi?

BIZTT

It's...she's outside.

Our life is getting really complicated.

Tell me about it.

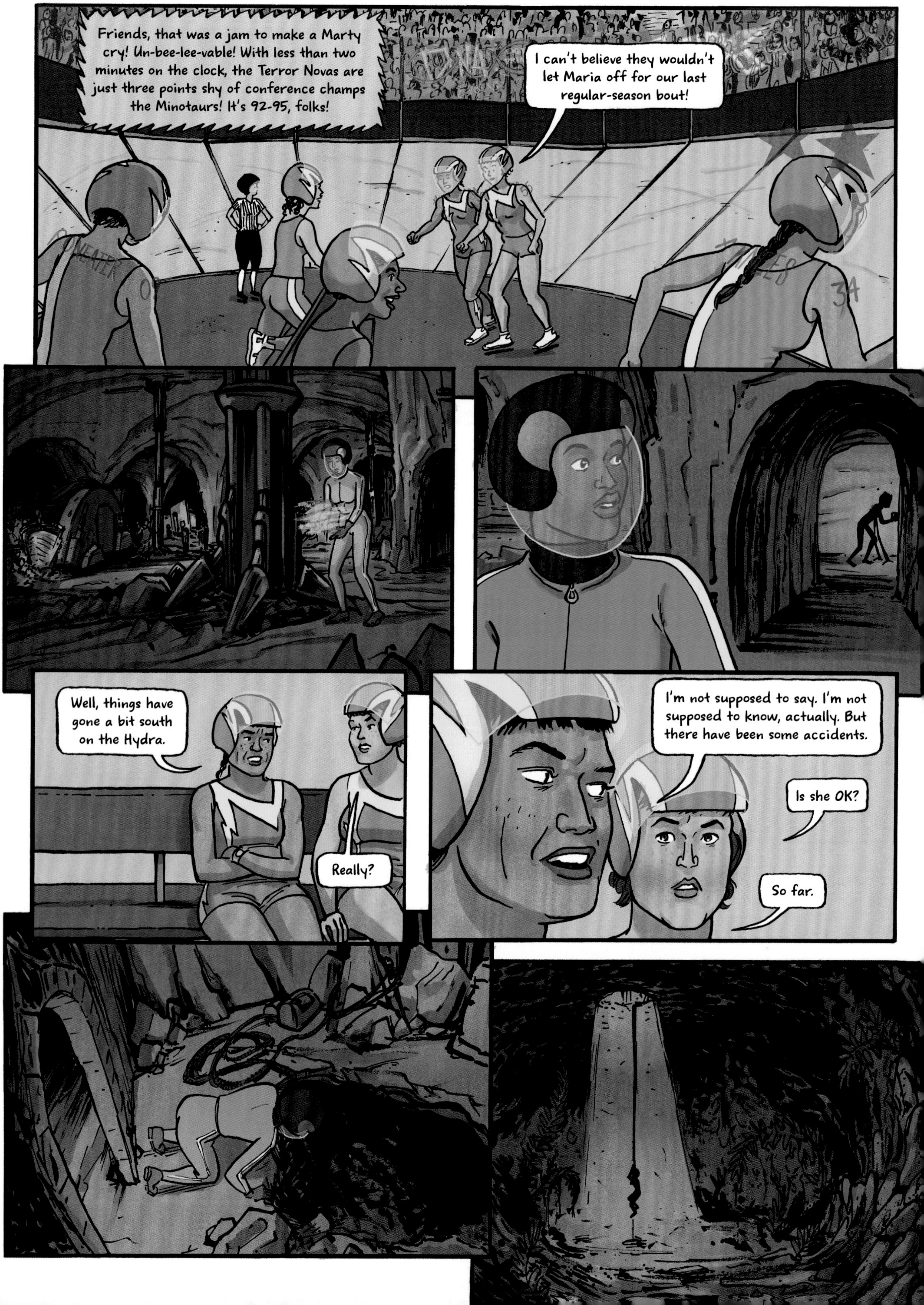
Friends, that was a jam to make a Marty cry! Un-bee-lee-vable! With less than two minutes on the clock, the Terror Novas are just three points shy of conference champs the Minotaurs! It's 92-95, folks!
I can't believe they wouldn't let Maria off for our last regular-season bout!
Well, things have gone a bit south on the Hydra.
Really?
I'm not supposed to say. I'm not supposed to know, actually. But there have been some accidents.
Is she OK?
So far.

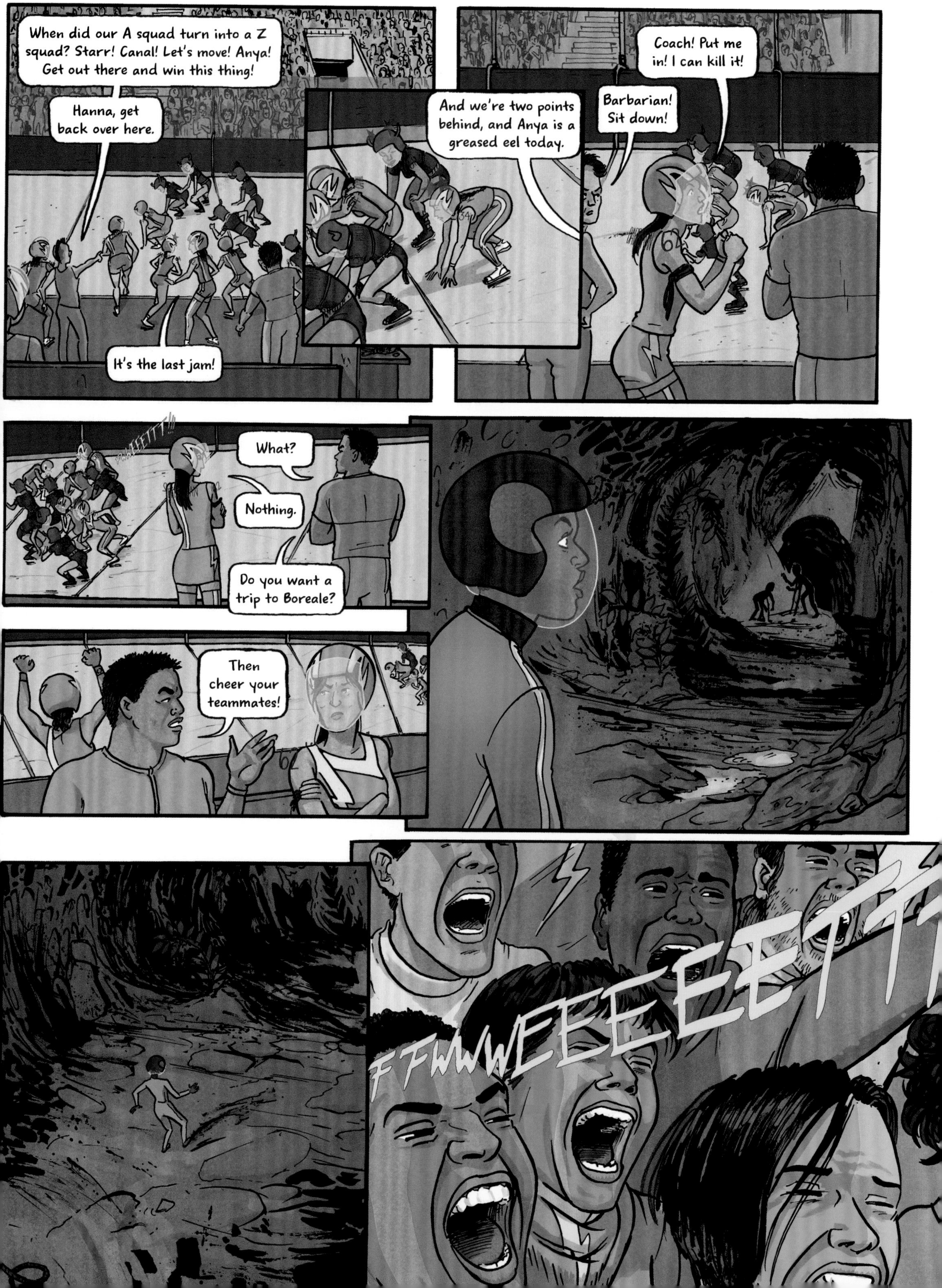
When did our A squad turn into a Z squad? Starr! Canal! Let's move! Anya! Get out there and win this thing!
Hanna, get back over here.
It's the last jam!
And we're two points behind, and Anya is a greased eel today.
Coach! Put me in! I can kill it!
Barbarian! Sit down!
FWWEEETTT!!
What?
Nothing.
Do you want a trip to Boreale?
Then cheer your teammates!
FFWWWEEEEEETTT

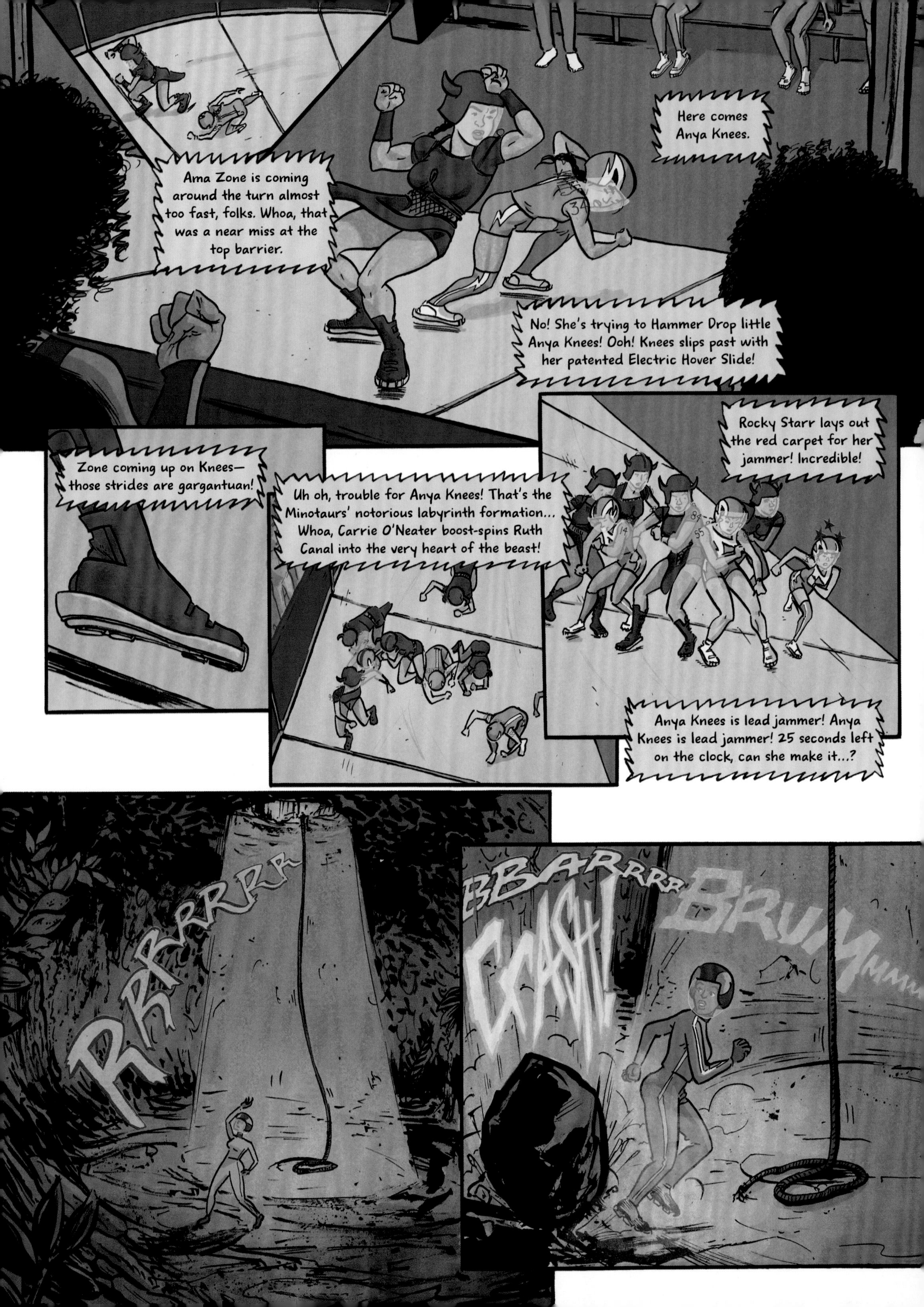
Ama Zone is coming around the turn almost too fast, folks. Whoa, that was a near miss at the top barrier.
Here comes Anya Knees.
No! She's trying to Hammer Drop little Anya Knees! Ooh! Knees slips past with her patented Electric Hover Slide!
Zone coming up on Knees—those strides are gargantuan!
Uh oh, trouble for Anya Knees! That's the Minotaurs' notorious labyrinth formation... Whoa, Carrie O'Neater boost-spins Ruth Canal into the very heart of the beast!
Rocky Starr lays out the red carpet for her jammer! Incredible!
Anya Knees is lead jammer! Anya Knees is lead jammer! 25 seconds left on the clock, can she make it...?
RRRRRRRRR
BBARRRRR
CRASH!
BRUM

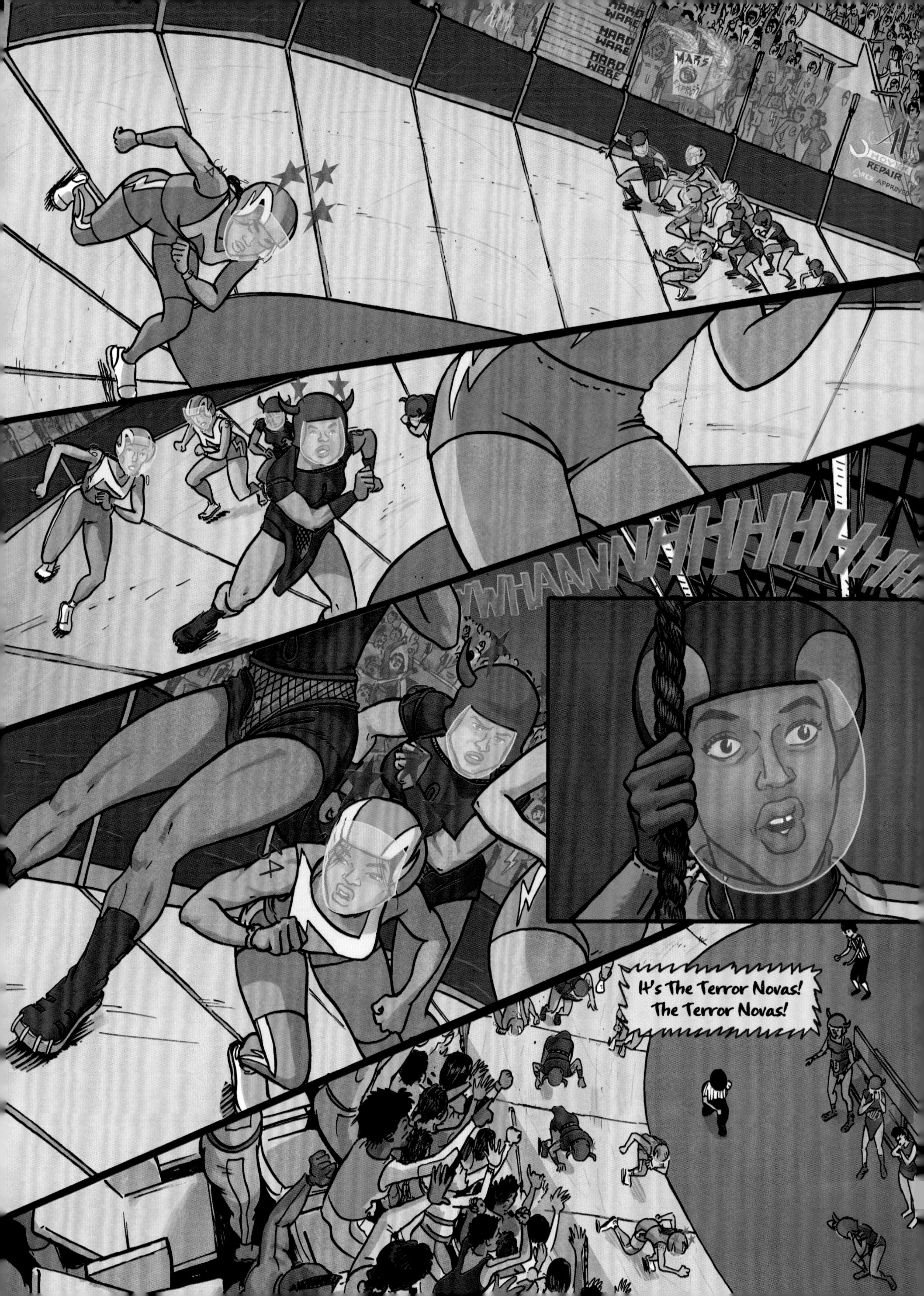
HARD WARE
HARD WARE
HARD WARE
MARS EXPRESS
HOVER REPAIR
AREX APPROVED
YWHAANNHHHHHHH
It's The Terror Novas! The Terror Novas!

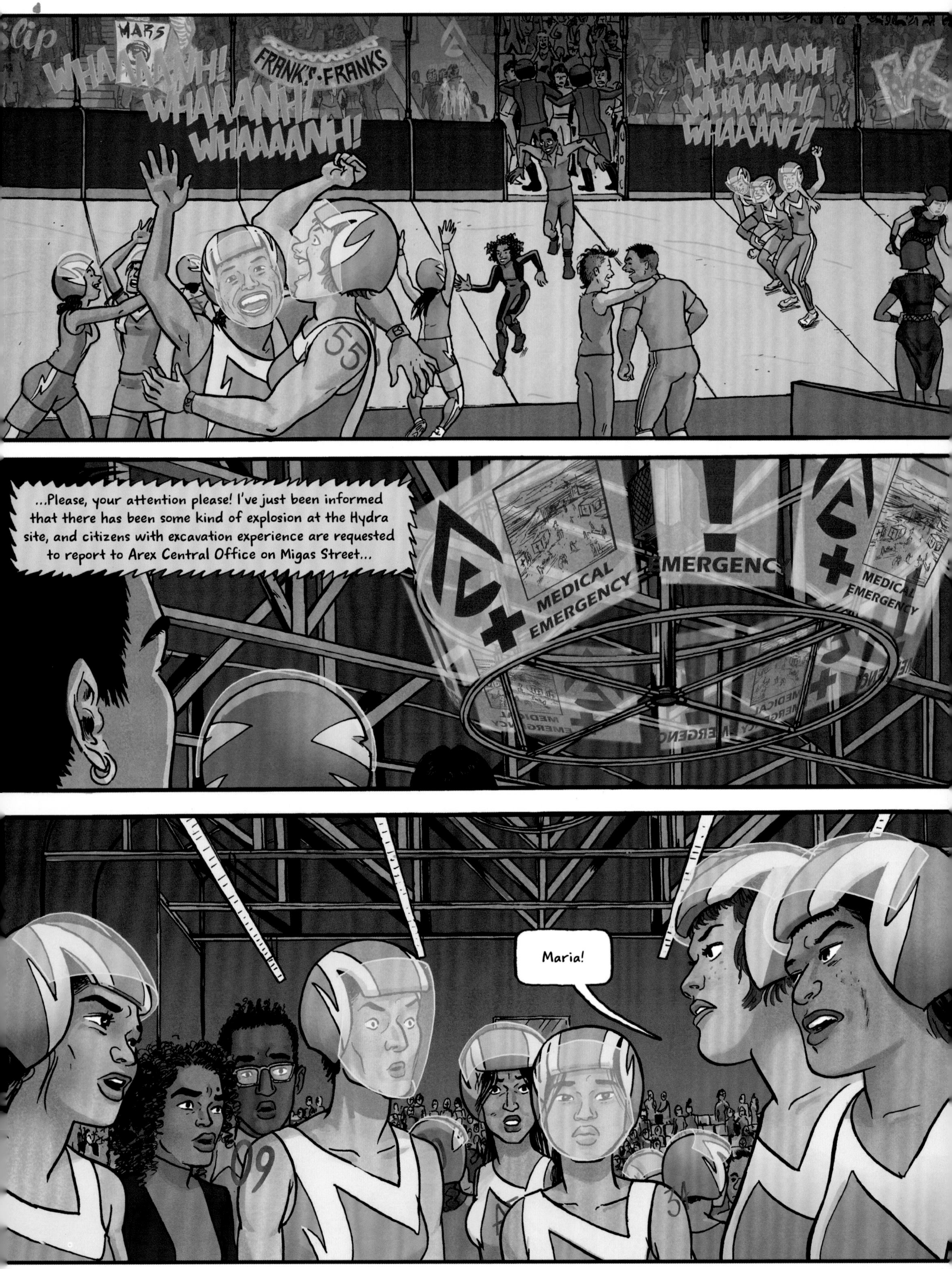
Slip
MARS
FRANK'S FRANKS
WHAAAANH!
WHAAANH!
WHAAAANH!
WHAAAANH!
WHAAANH!
WHAAANH!
...Please, your attention please! I've just been informed that there has been some kind of explosion at the Hydra site, and citizens with excavation experience are requested to report to Arex Central Office on Migas Street...
MEDICAL EMERGENCY
EMERGENCY
MEDICAL EMERGENCY
Maria!

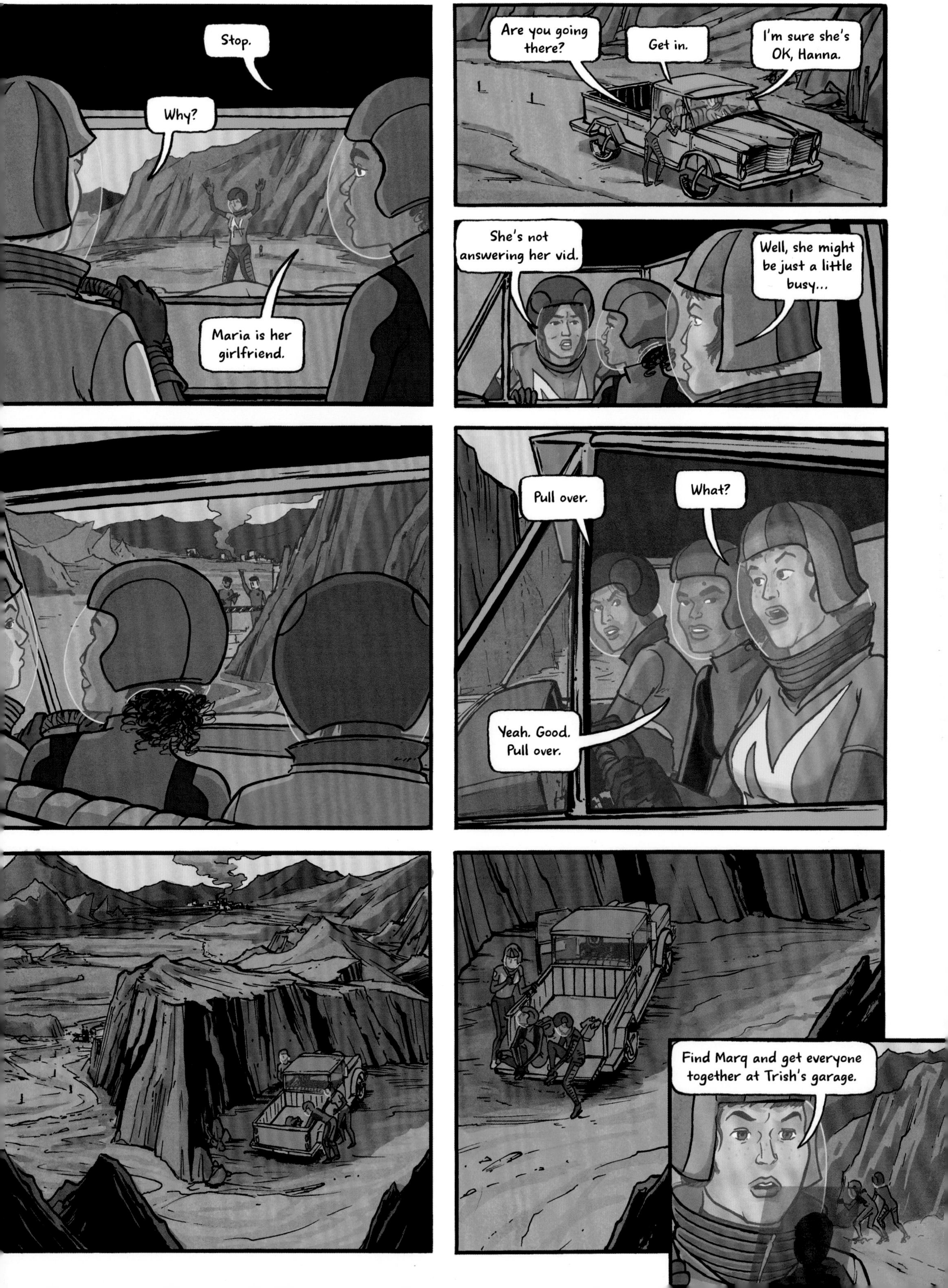
Stop.
Why?
Maria is her girlfriend.
Are you going there?
Get in.
I'm sure she's OK, Hanna.
She's not answering her vid.
Well, she might be just a little busy...
Pull over.
What?
Yeah. Good. Pull over.
Find Marq and get everyone together at Trish's garage.

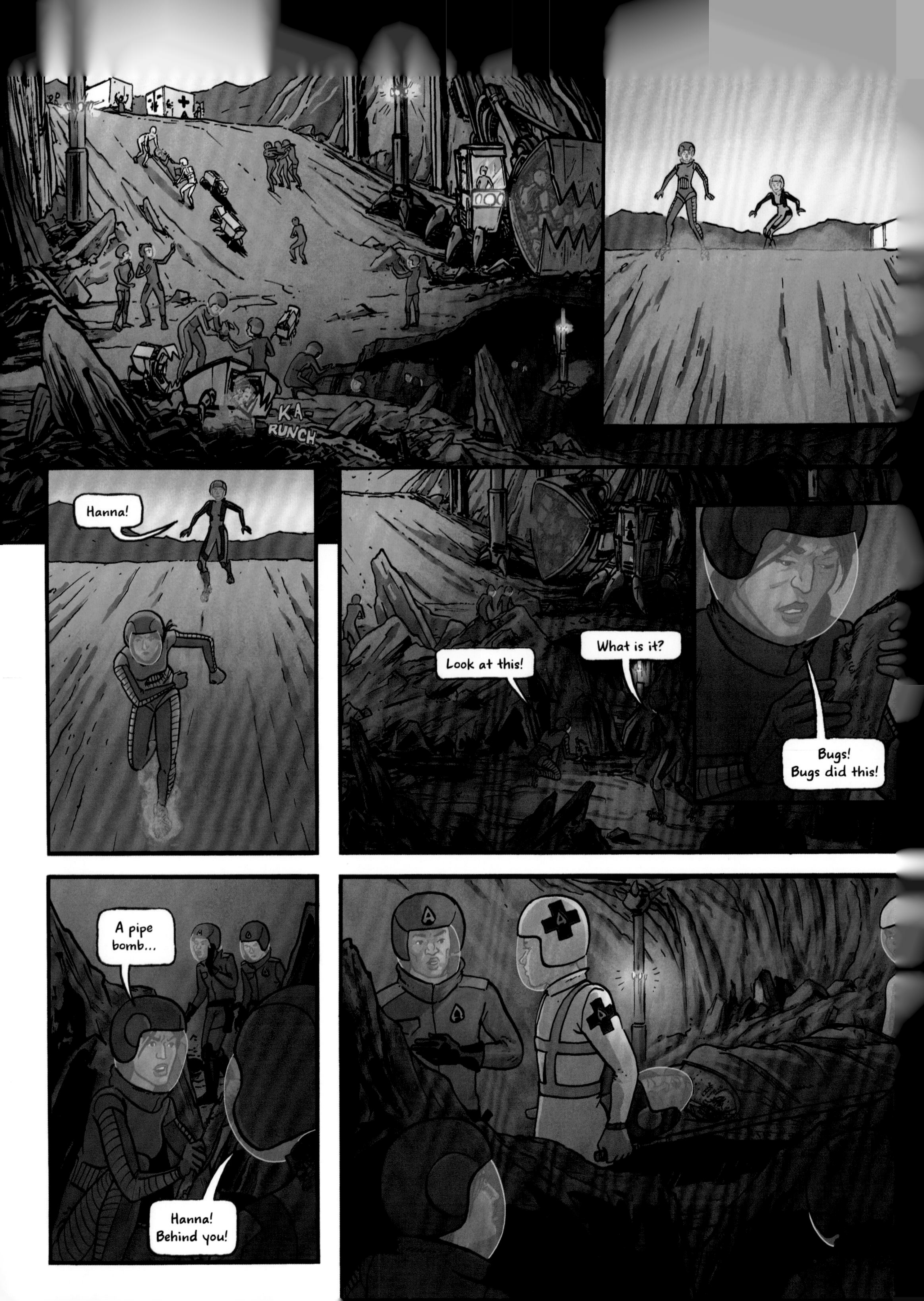
KA-RUNCH
Hanna!
Look at this!
What is it?
Bugs! Bugs did this!
A pipe bomb...
Hanna! Behind you!

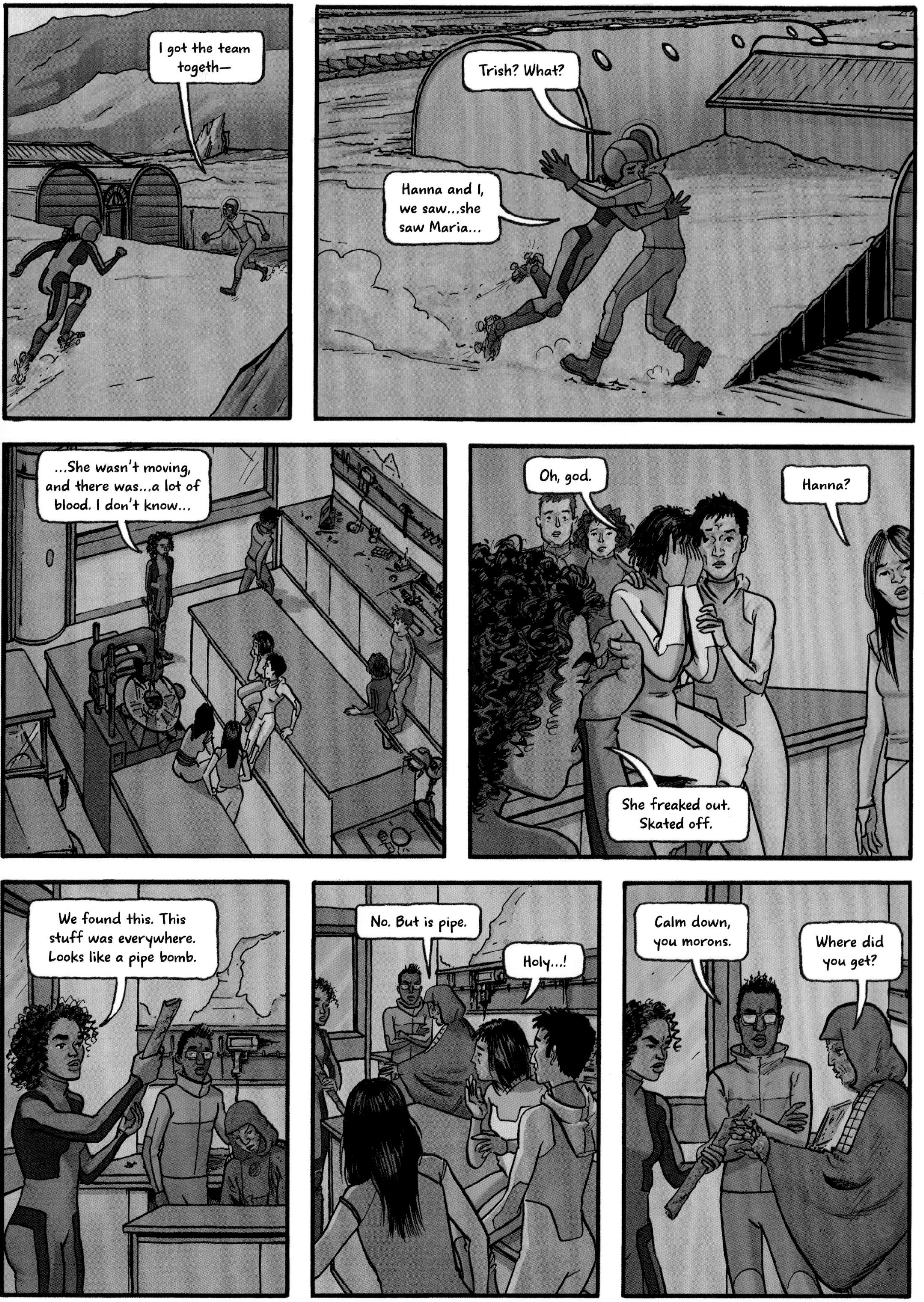
I got the team togeth—
Trish? What?
Hanna and I, we saw...she saw Maria...
...She wasn't moving, and there was...a lot of blood. I don't know...
Oh, god.
Hanna?
She freaked out. Skated off.
We found this. This stuff was everywhere. Looks like a pipe bomb.
No. But is pipe.
Holy...!
Calm down, you morons.
Where did you get?

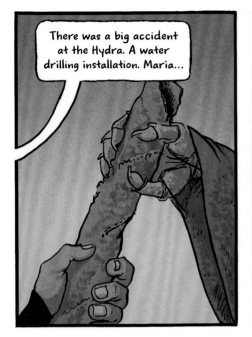

There was a big accident at the Hydra. A water drilling installation. Maria...

That is what they came for. Now I see.

Qiqi?

My nest, other nest work-kt together. Not usual. Your "Hydra" is on top of thkilsktilktkt...the reservoir, you would say. My nest is caretaker. Clans came to move the water to a safe place.

What are you talking about?

The Hydra. There's no natural aquifer. There *was* a *reservoir.* Which is now empty.

Was a natural aquifer, many, many cycles past. But water is precious to us, holy. We guard and keep it. Long ago, we gathered that water and made a holy place. I hear talking—elders worried Terrans will find. But if the water is gone...

The structure will collapse.

You mean your people hoard water while we die of thirst?

They...we do this. It is not right, but...

I should not think "I" and "they": I am bad, I am broken.

Qiqi, it's not your fault...

What the hell, Marq? If it's not her fault, then whose...

Carrie, it's...

Trisha, I need to talk to you.

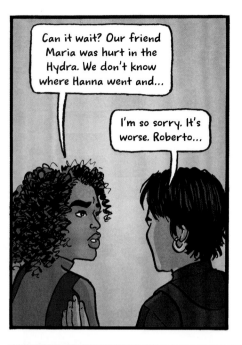

Can it wait? Our friend Maria was hurt in the Hydra. We don't know where Hanna went and...

I'm so sorry. It's worse. Roberto...

Tía, what?

He's dead.

No! What?! NO!

He was on a small reconnaissance ship in the Kuiper Belt. Hit by an asteroid fragment.

No! It's my fault! He would never have been up there if it weren't for me!

No.

No.

49

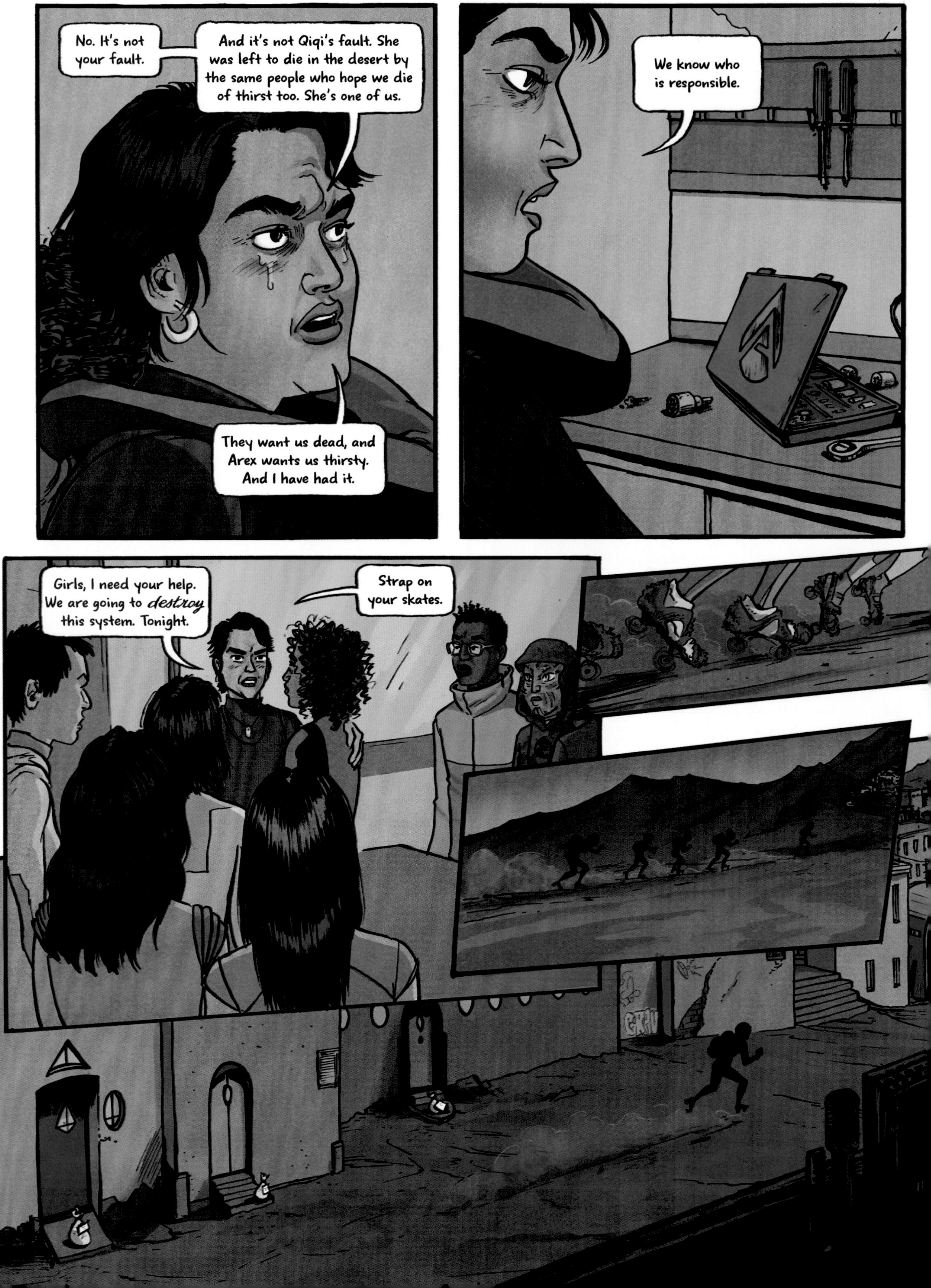
No. It's not your fault.
And it's not Qiqi's fault. She was left to die in the desert by the same people who hope we die of thirst too. She's one of us.
They want us dead, and Arex wants us thirsty. And I have had it.
We know who is responsible.
Girls, I need your help. We are going to *destroy* this system. Tonight.
Strap on your skates.

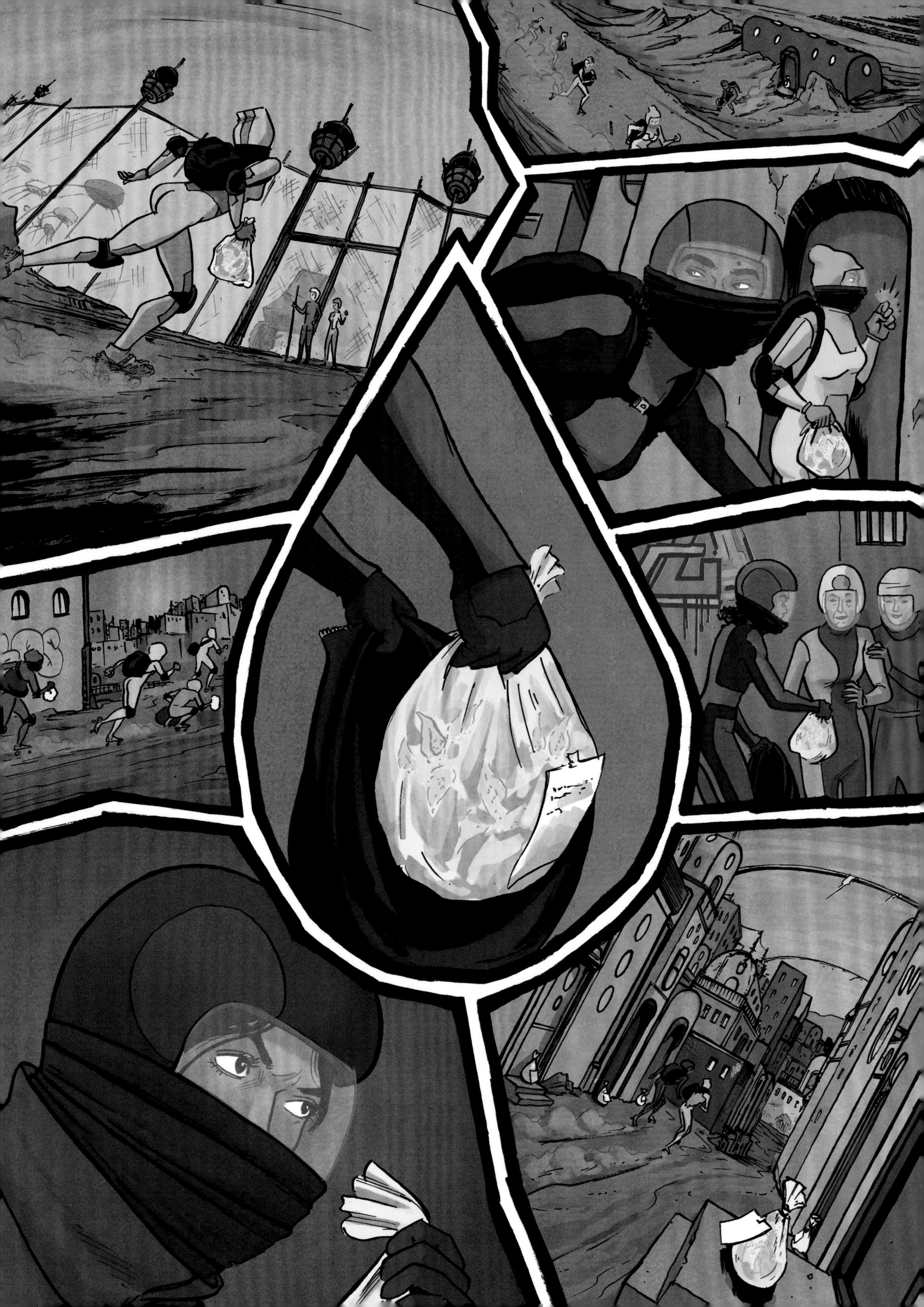

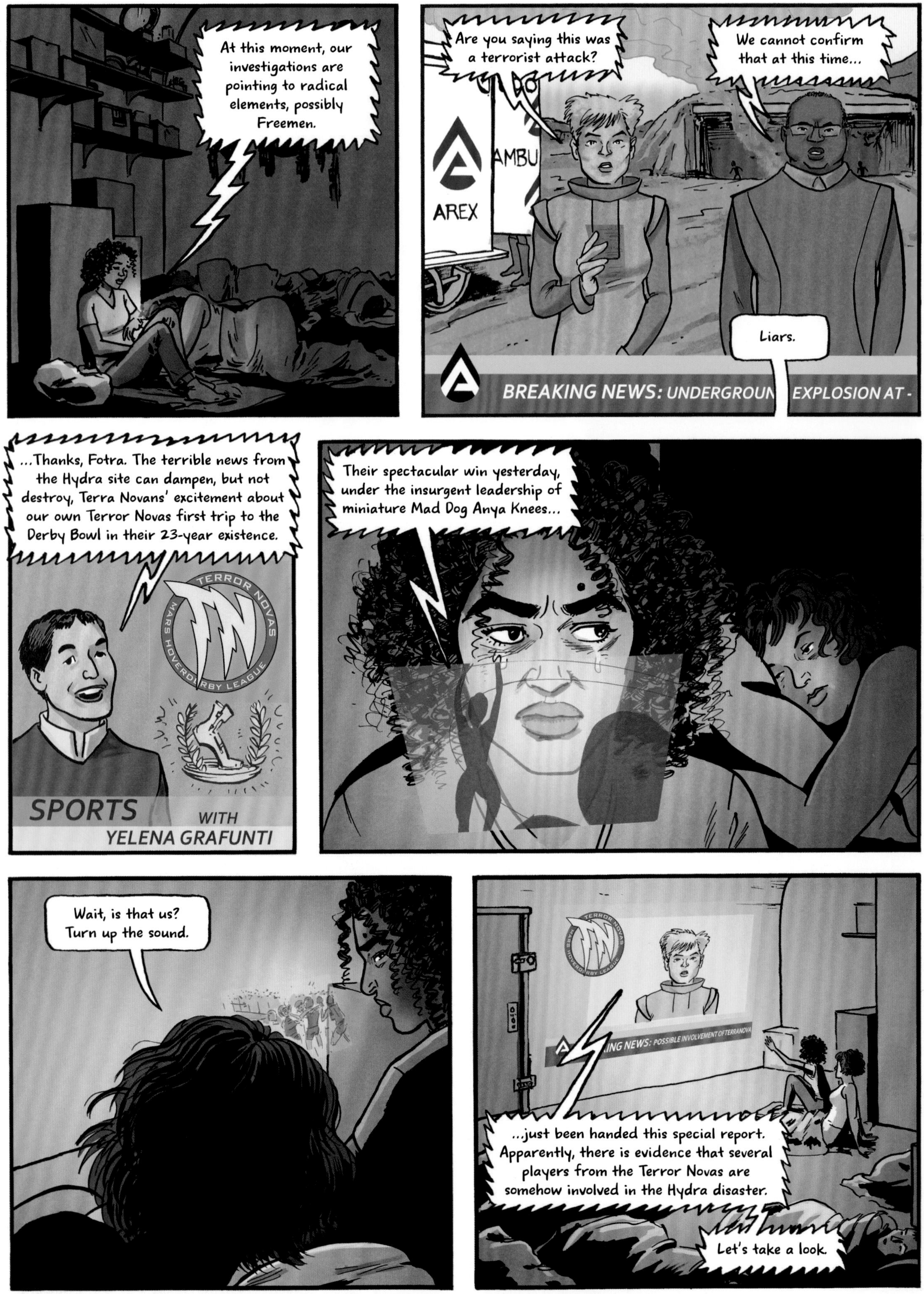
At this moment, our investigations are pointing to radical elements, possibly Freemen.
Are you saying this was a terrorist attack?
We cannot confirm that at this time...
AMBU
AREX
Liars.
BREAKING NEWS: UNDERGROUN EXPLOSION AT -
...Thanks, Fotra. The terrible news from the Hydra site can dampen, but not destroy, Terra Novans' excitement about our own Terror Novas first trip to the Derby Bowl in their 23-year existence.
TERROR NOVAS
MARS HOVERDARBY LEAGUE
SPORTS WITH YELENA GRAFUNTI
Their spectacular win yesterday, under the insurgent leadership of miniature Mad Dog Anya Knees...
Wait, is that us? Turn up the sound.
ING NEWS: POSSIBLE INVOLVEMENT OFTERRANOVA
...just been handed this special report. Apparently, there is evidence that several players from the Terror Novas are somehow involved in the Hydra disaster.
Let's take a look.

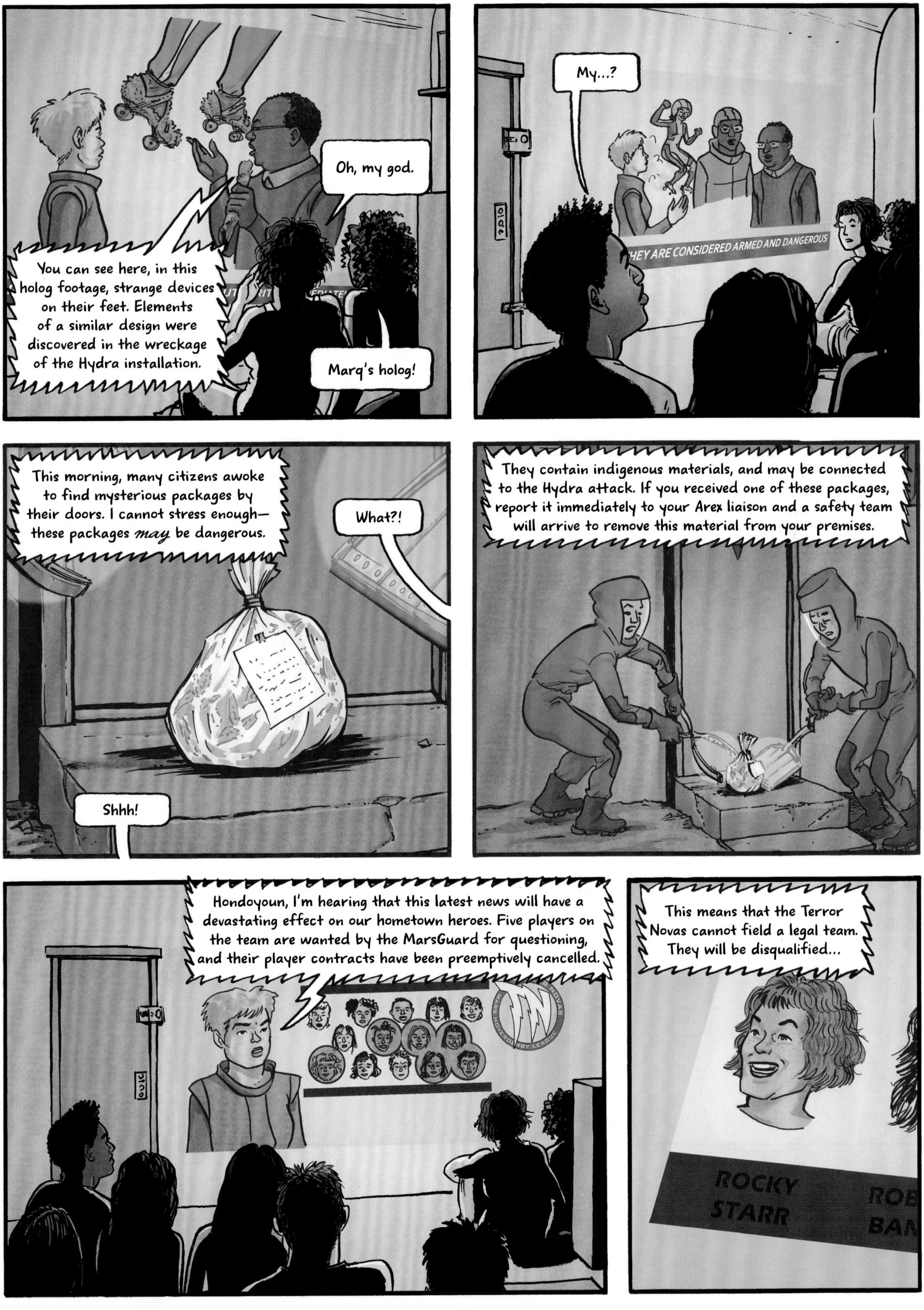
Oh, my god.
You can see here, in this holog footage, strange devices on their feet. Elements of a similar design were discovered in the wreckage of the Hydra installation.
Marq's holog!
My...?
THEY ARE CONSIDERED ARMED AND DANGEROUS
This morning, many citizens awoke to find mysterious packages by their doors. I cannot stress enough—these packages *may* be dangerous.
What?!
Shhh!
They contain indigenous materials, and may be connected to the Hydra attack. If you received one of these packages, report it immediately to your Arex liaison and a safety team will arrive to remove this material from your premises.
Hondoyoun, I'm hearing that this latest news will have a devastating effect on our hometown heroes. Five players on the team are wanted by the MarsGuard for questioning, and their player contracts have been preemptively cancelled.
This means that the Terror Novas cannot field a legal team. They will be disqualified...
ROCKY STARR

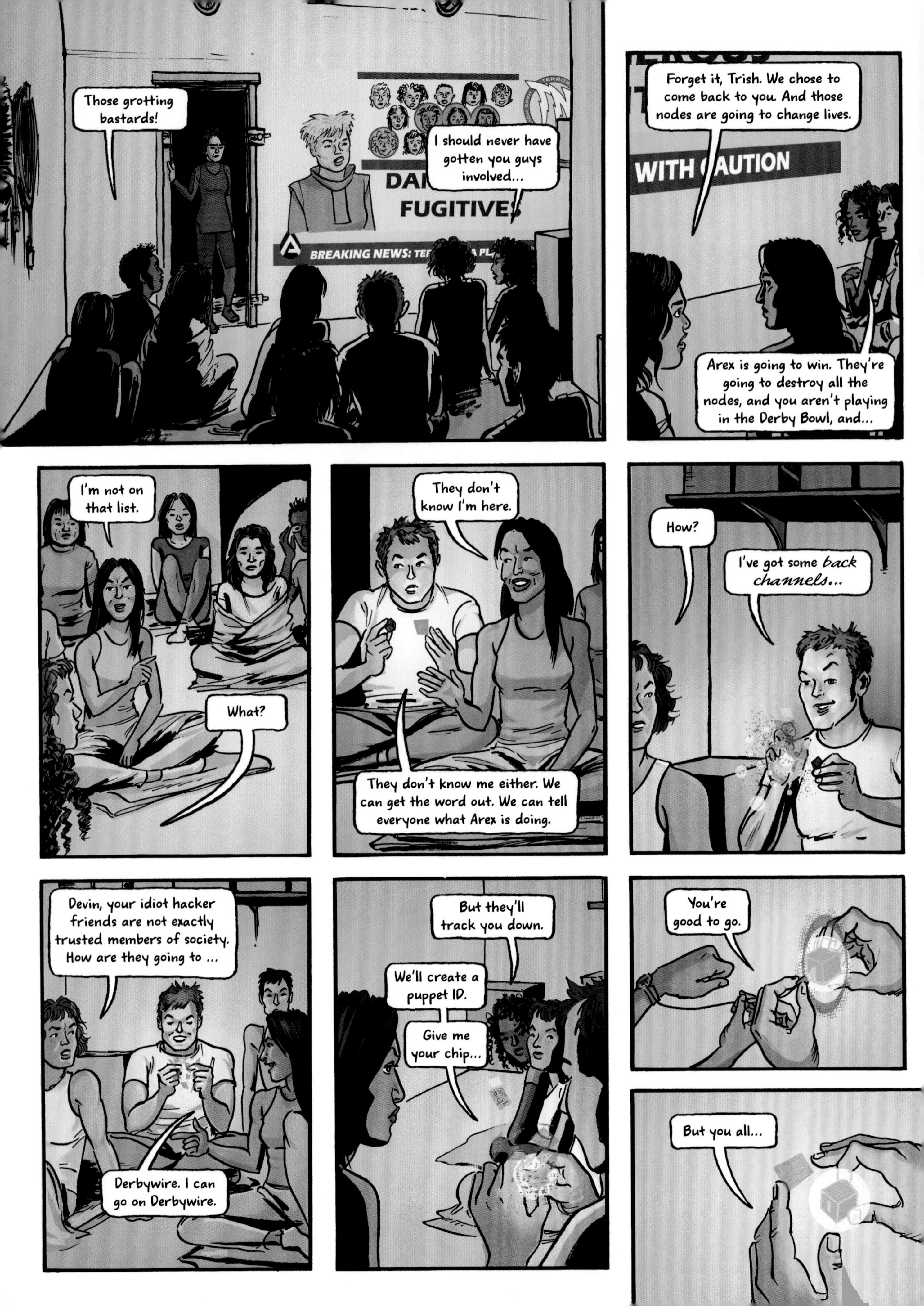

DANGEROUS FUGITIVES
BREAKING NEWS:
Those grotting bastards!
I should never have gotten you guys involved...
WITH CAUTION
Forget it, Trish. We chose to come back to you. And those nodes are going to change lives.
Arex is going to win. They're going to destroy all the nodes, and you aren't playing in the Derby Bowl, and...
I'm not on that list.
What?
They don't know I'm here.
They don't know me either. We can get the word out. We can tell everyone what Arex is doing.
How?
I've got some *back channels...*
Devin, your idiot hacker friends are not exactly trusted members of society. How are they going to ...
Derbywire. I can go on Derbywire.
But they'll track you down.
We'll create a puppet ID.
Give me your chip...
You're good to go.
But you all...

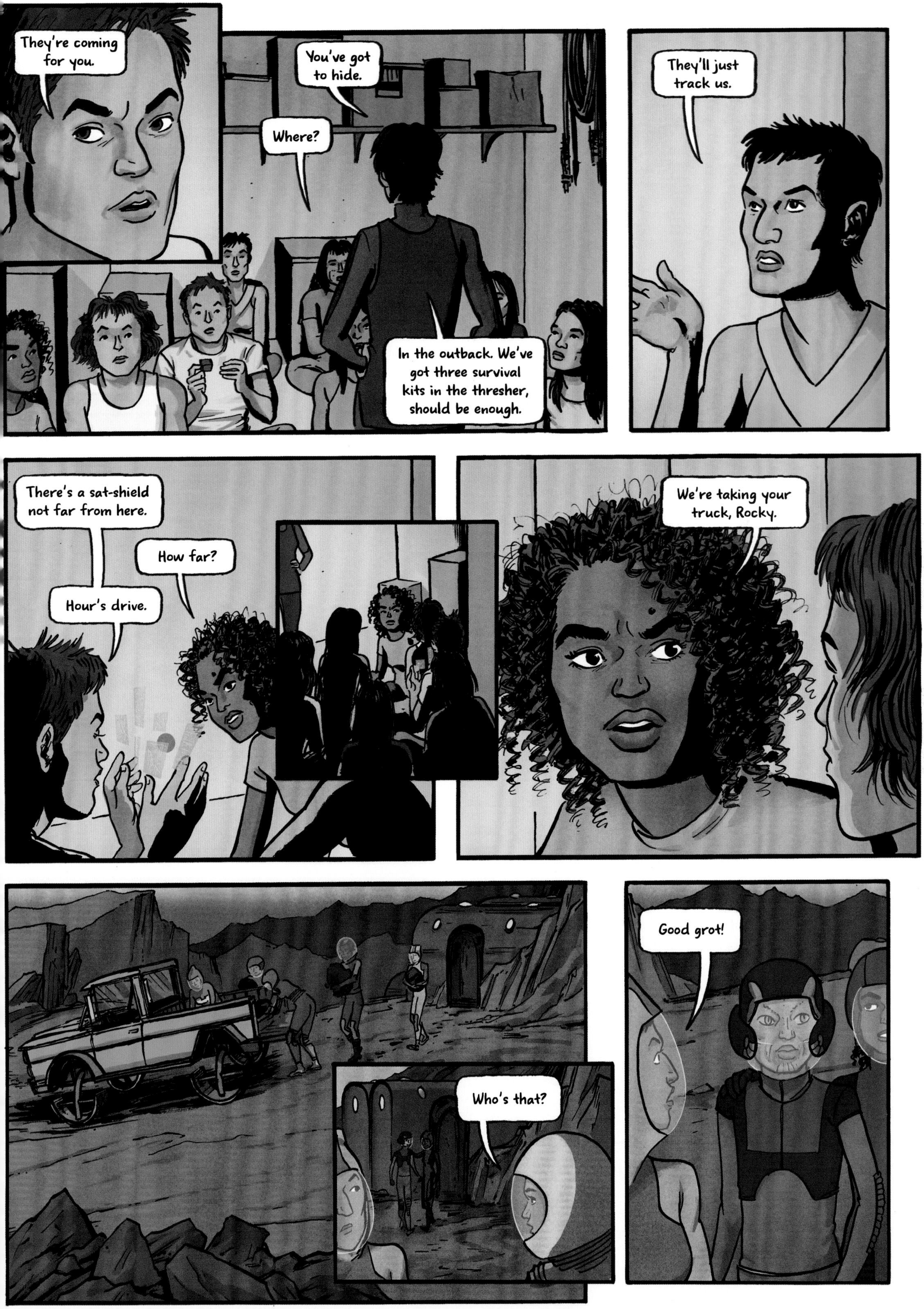
They're coming for you.
You've got to hide.
Where?
In the outback. We've got three survival kits in the thresher, should be enough.
They'll just track us.
There's a sat-shield not far from here.
How far?
Hour's drive.
We're taking your truck, Rocky.
Who's that?
Good grot!

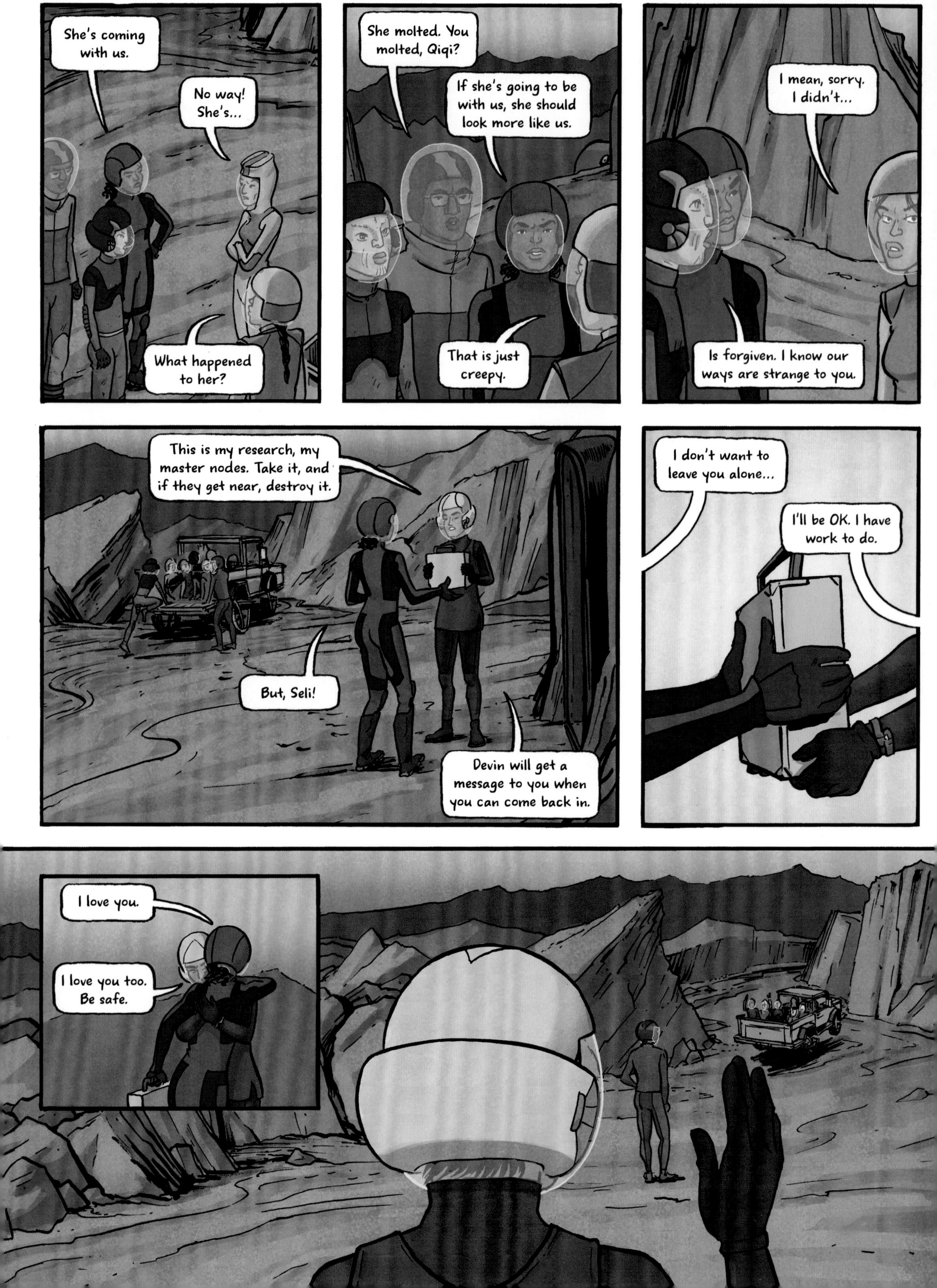
She's coming with us.
No way! She's...
What happened to her?
She molted. You molted, Qiqi?
If she's going to be with us, she should look more like us.
That is just creepy.
I mean, sorry. I didn't...
Is forgiven. I know our ways are strange to you.
This is my research, my master nodes. Take it, and if they get near, destroy it.
But, Seli!
Devin will get a message to you when you can come back in.
I don't want to leave you alone...
I'll be OK. I have work to do.
I love you.
I love you too. Be safe.

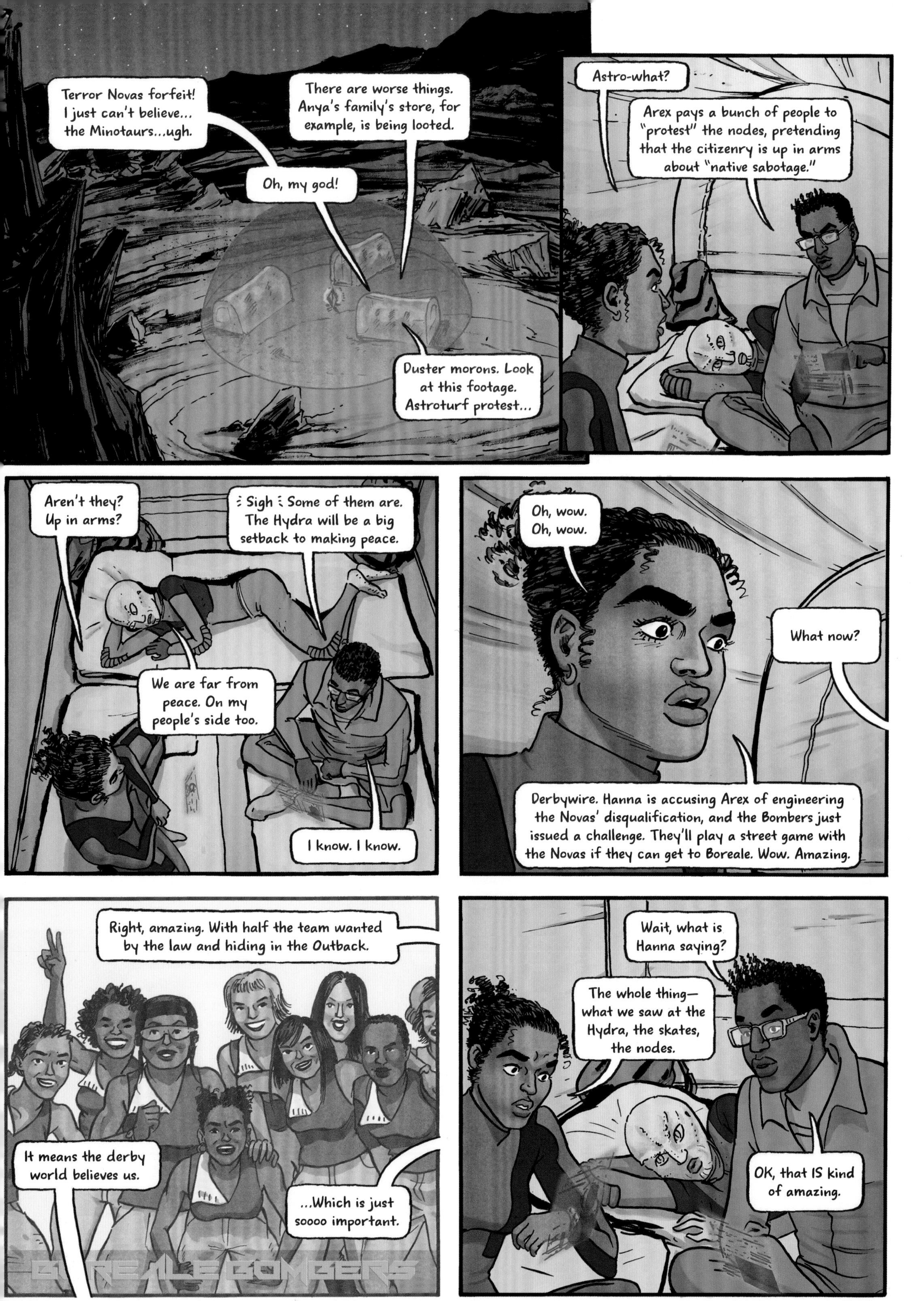
Terror Novas forfeit! I just can't believe... the Minotaurs...ugh.
There are worse things. Anya's family's store, for example, is being looted.
Oh, my god!
Duster morons. Look at this footage. Astroturf protest...
Astro-what?
Arex pays a bunch of people to "protest" the nodes, pretending that the citizenry is up in arms about "native sabotage."
Aren't they? Up in arms?
⁝ Sigh ⁝ Some of them are. The Hydra will be a big setback to making peace.
We are far from peace. On my people's side too.
I know. I know.
Oh, wow. Oh, wow.
What now?
Derbywire. Hanna is accusing Arex of engineering the Novas' disqualification, and the Bombers just issued a challenge. They'll play a street game with the Novas if they can get to Boreale. Wow. Amazing.
Right, amazing. With half the team wanted by the law and hiding in the Outback.
It means the derby world believes us.
...Which is just soooo important.
Wait, what is Hanna saying?
The whole thing—what we saw at the Hydra, the skates, the nodes.
OK, that IS kind of amazing.

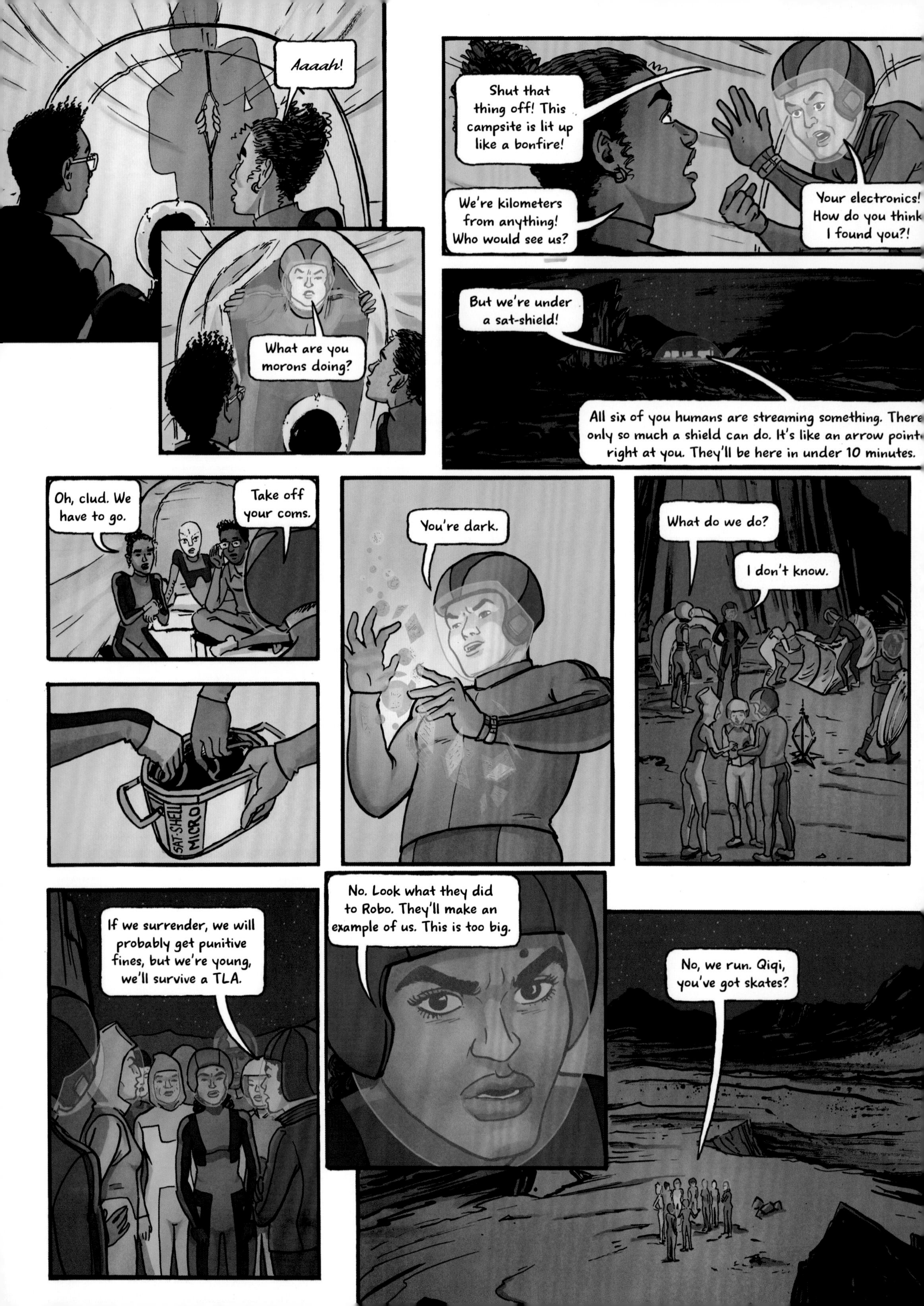

Aaaah!
What are you morons doing?
Shut that thing off! This campsite is lit up like a bonfire!
We're kilometers from anything! Who would see us?
Your electronics! How do you think I found you?!
But we're under a sat-shield!
All six of you humans are streaming something. There only so much a shield can do. It's like an arrow point right at you. They'll be here in under 10 minutes.
Oh, clud. We have to go.
Take off your coms.
SAT-SHELL MICRO
You're dark.
What do we do?
I don't know.
If we surrender, we will probably get punitive fines, but we're young, we'll survive a TLA.
No. Look what they did to Robo. They'll make an example of us. This is too big.
No, we run. Qiqi, you've got skates?

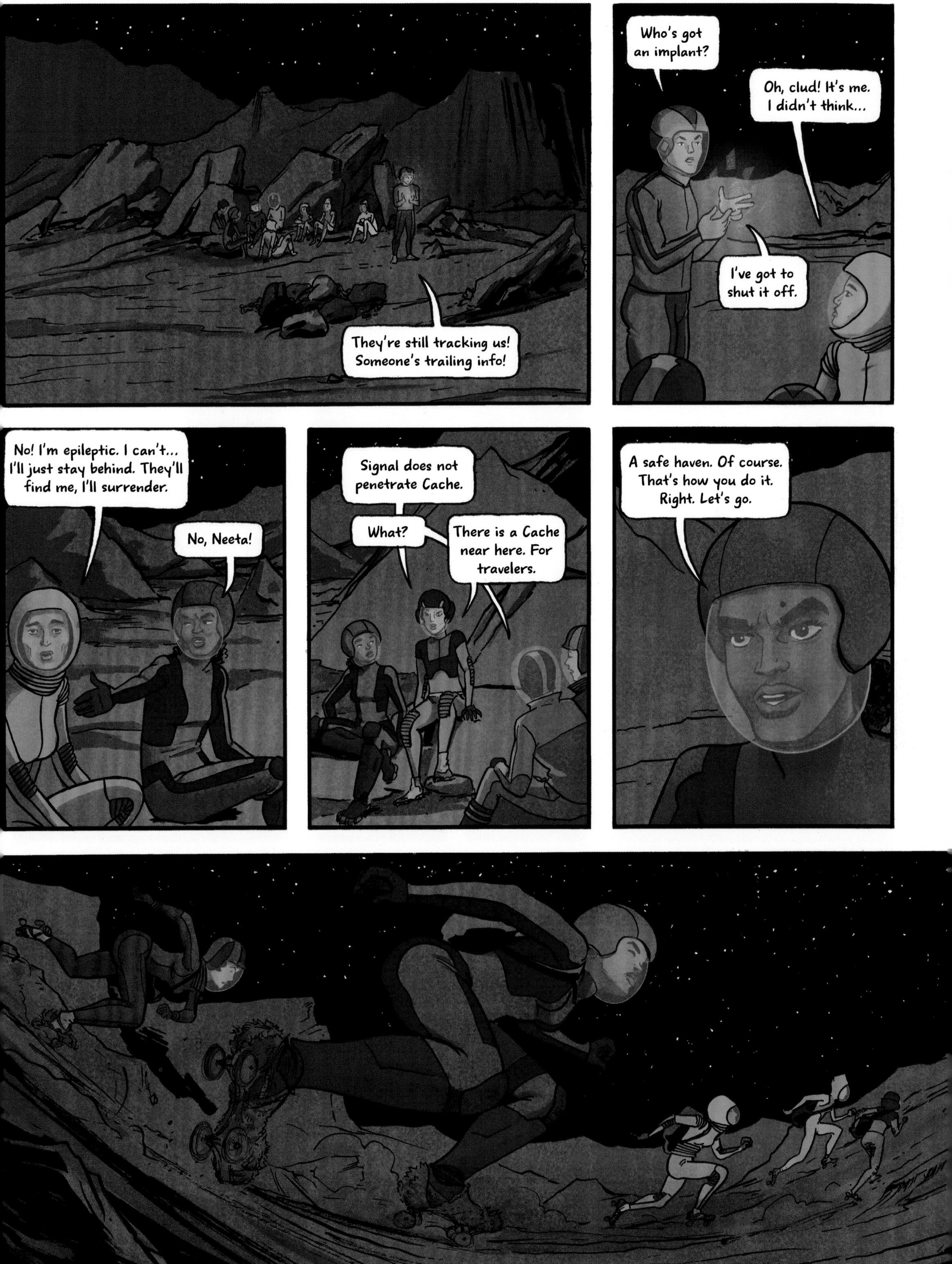
They're still tracking us! Someone's trailing info!
Who's got an implant?
Oh, clud! It's me. I didn't think...
I've got to shut it off.
No! I'm epileptic. I can't... I'll just stay behind. They'll find me, I'll surrender.
No, Neeta!
Signal does not penetrate Cache.
What?
There is a Cache near here. For travelers.
A safe haven. Of course. That's how you do it. Right. Let's go.

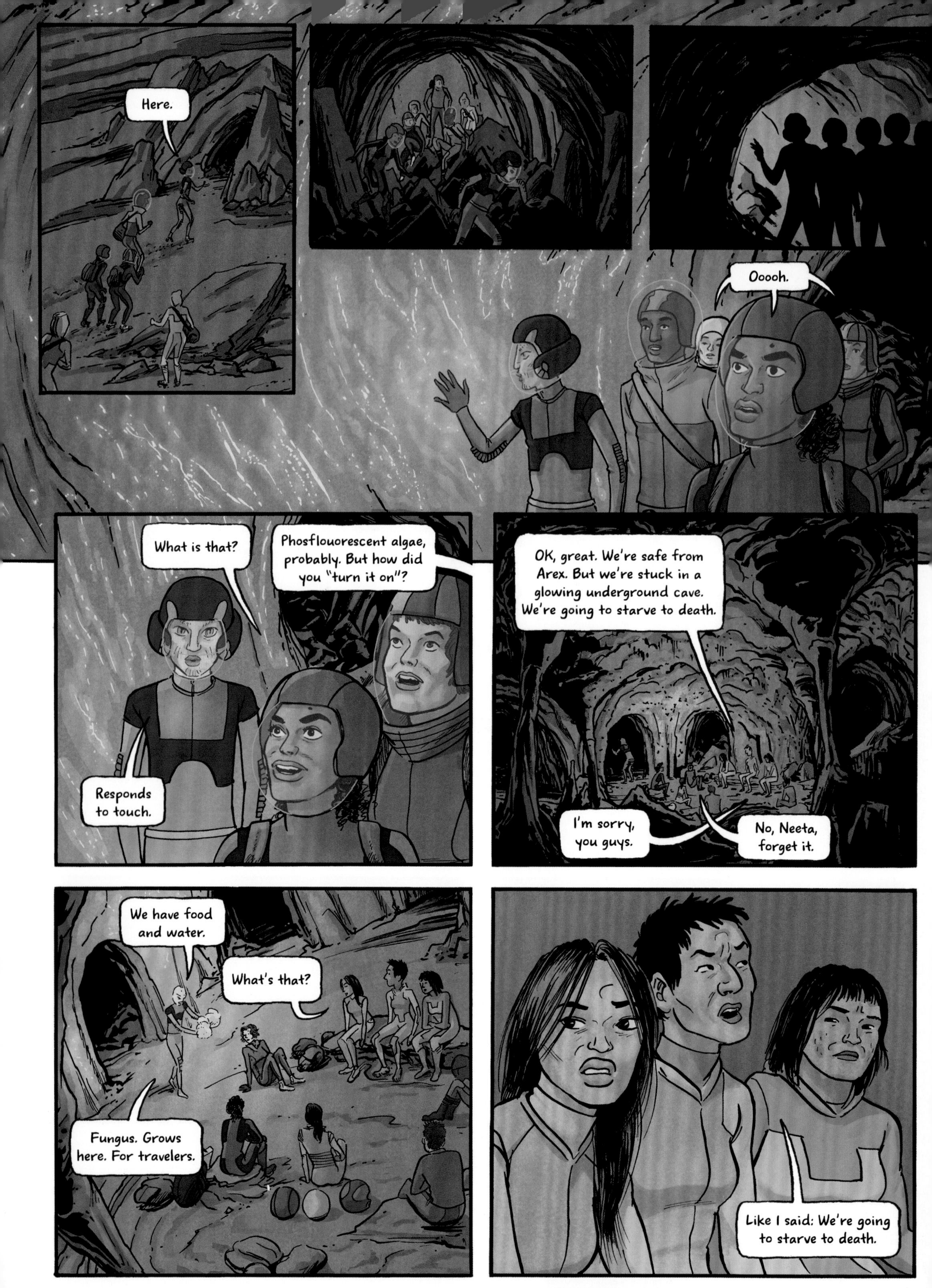
Here.
Ooooh.
What is that?
Phosflouorescent algae, probably. But how did you "turn it on"?
Responds to touch.
OK, great. We're safe from Arex. But we're stuck in a glowing underground cave. We're going to starve to death.
I'm sorry, you guys.
No, Neeta, forget it.
We have food and water.
What's that?
Fungus. Grows here. For travelers.
Like I said: We're going to starve to death.

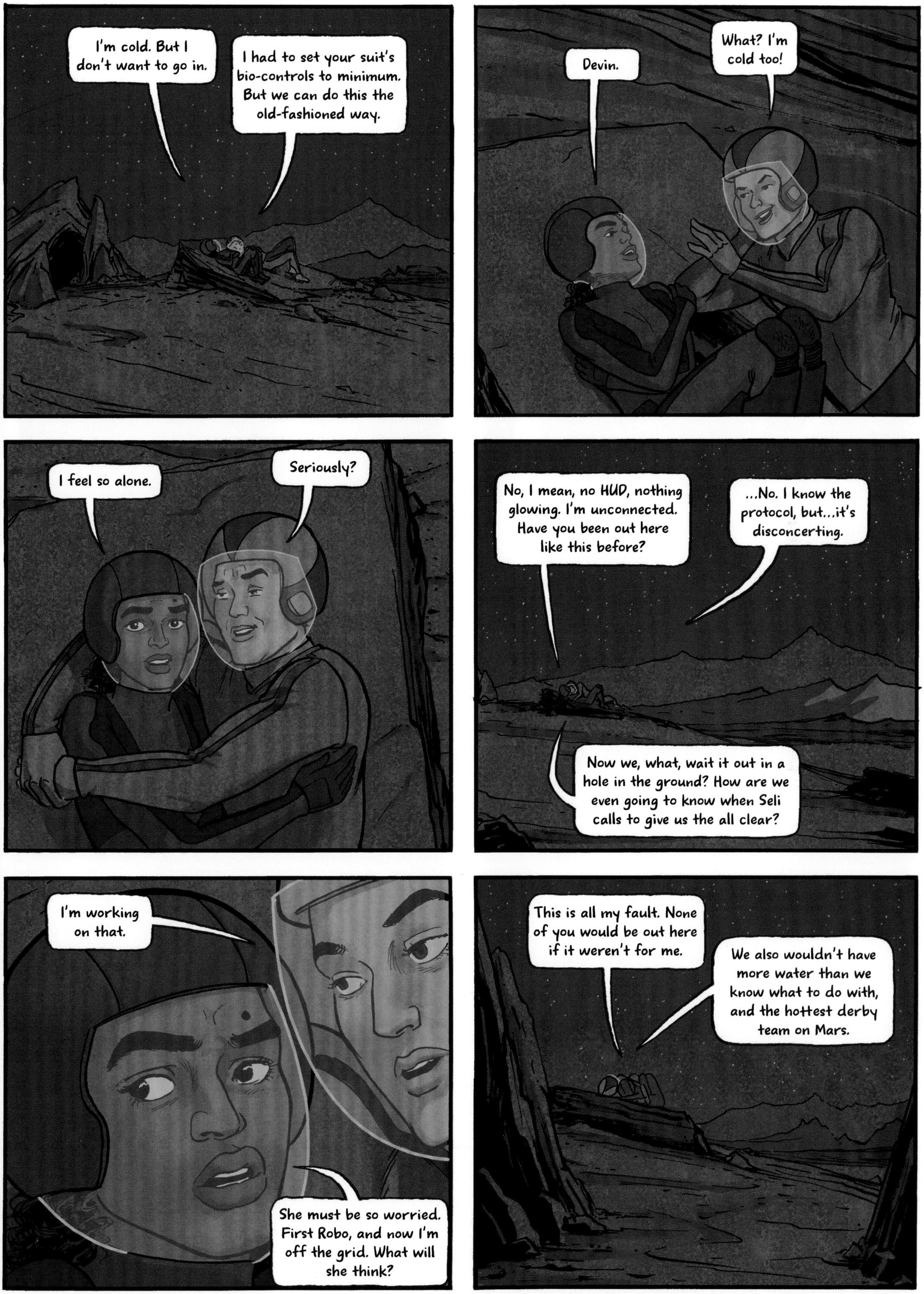
I'm cold. But I don't want to go in.
I had to set your suit's bio-controls to minimum. But we can do this the old-fashioned way.
Devin.
What? I'm cold too!
I feel so alone.
Seriously?
No, I mean, no HUD, nothing glowing. I'm unconnected. Have you been out here like this before?
...No. I know the protocol, but...it's disconcerting.
Now we, what, wait it out in a hole in the ground? How are we even going to know when Seli calls to give us the all clear?
I'm working on that.
She must be so worried. First Robo, and now I'm off the grid. What will she think?
This is all my fault. None of you would be out here if it weren't for me.
We also wouldn't have more water than we know what to do with, and the hottest derby team on Mars.

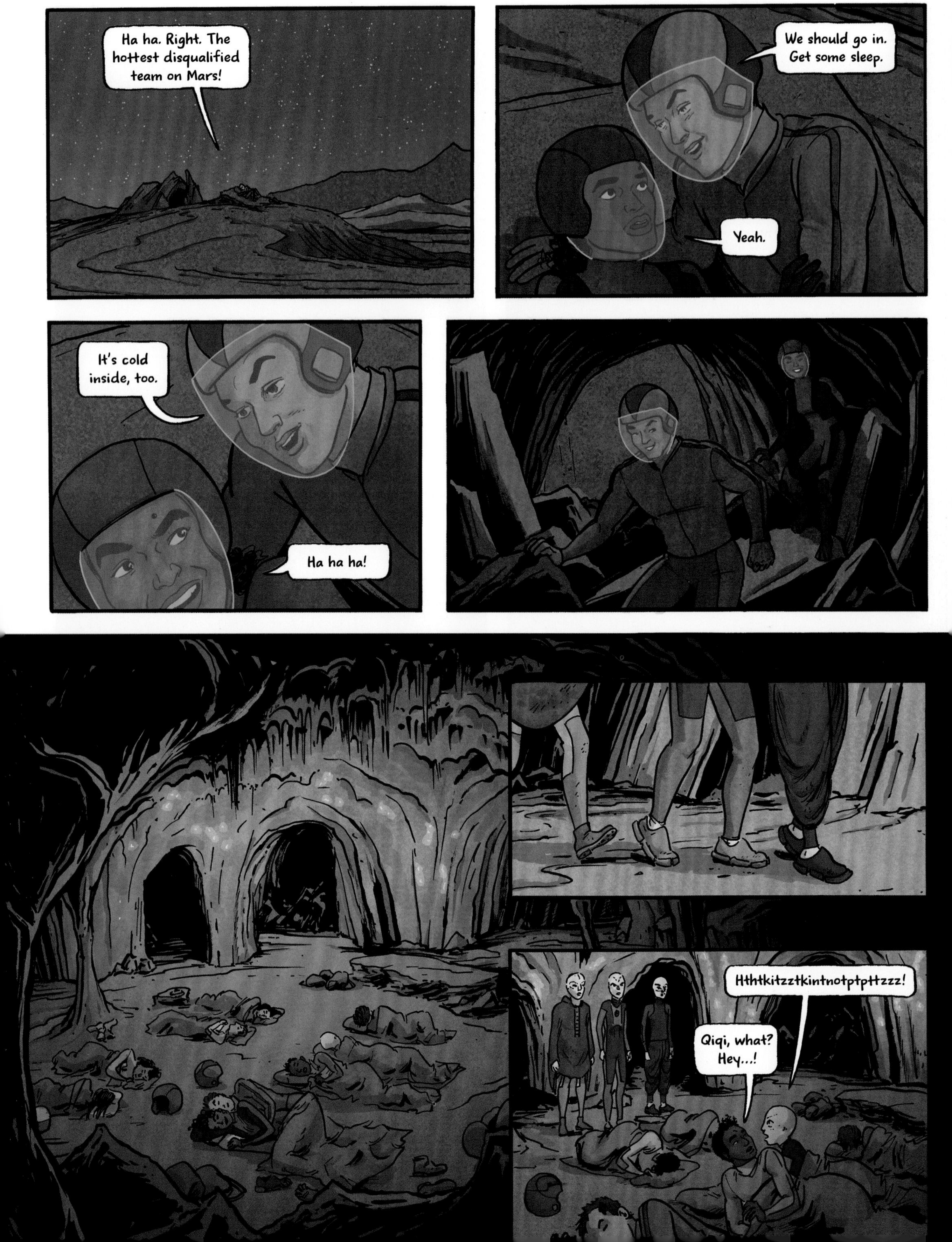
Ha ha. Right. The hottest disqualified team on Mars!
We should go in. Get some sleep.
Yeah.
It's cold inside, too.
Ha ha ha!
Hthtkitzztkintnotptptzzz!
Qiqi, what? Hey...!

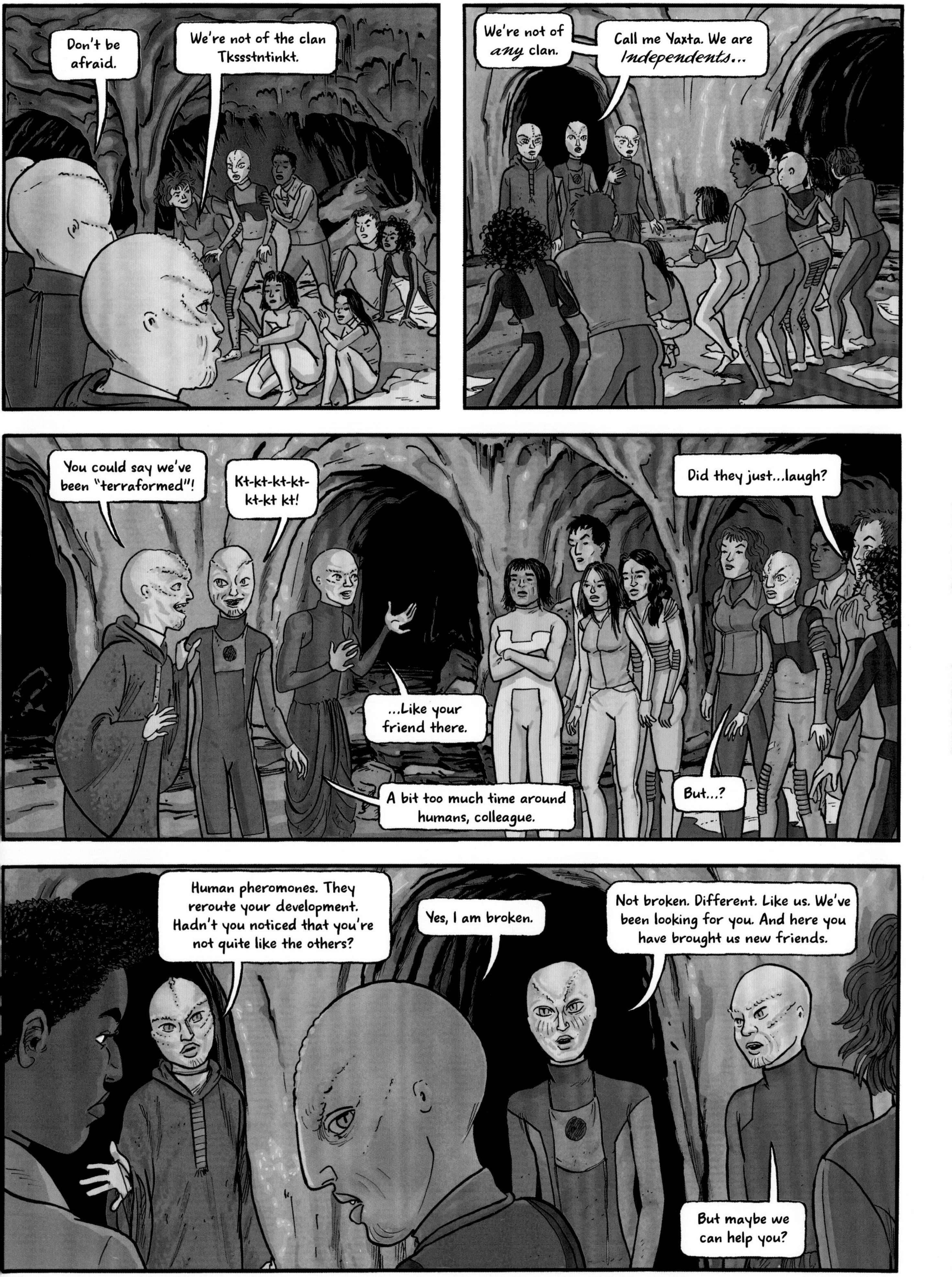
Don't be afraid.
We're not of the clan Tkssstntinkt.
We're not of *any* clan.
Call me Yaxta. We are *Independents...*
You could say we've been "terraformed"!
Kt-kt-kt-kt-kt-kt kt!
...Like your friend there.
A bit too much time around humans, colleague.
Did they just...laugh?
But...?
Human pheromones. They reroute your development. Hadn't you noticed that you're not quite like the others?
Yes, I am broken.
Not broken. Different. Like us. We've been looking for you. And here you have brought us new friends.
But maybe we can help you?

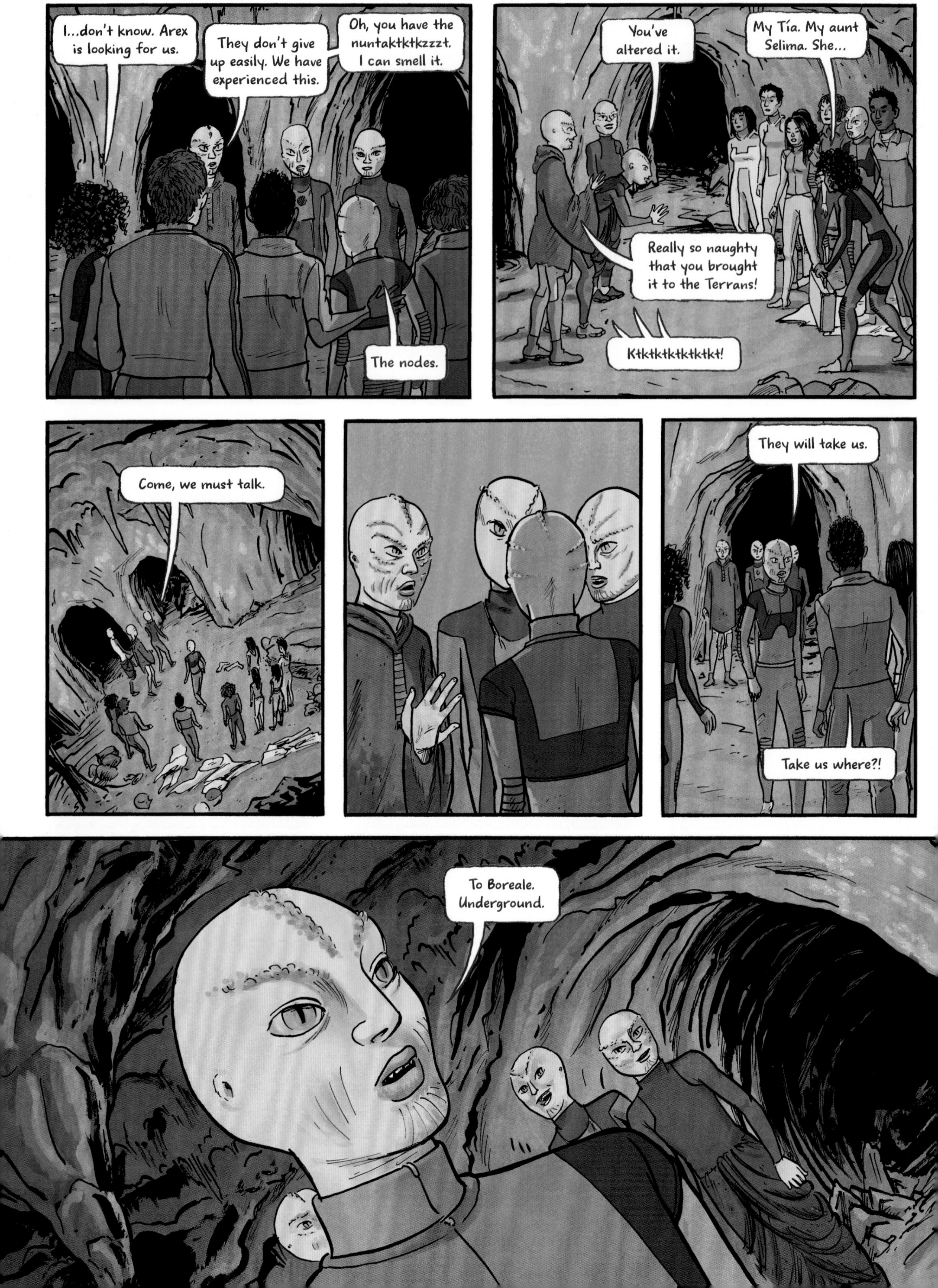
I...don't know. Arex is looking for us.
They don't give up easily. We have experienced this.
Oh, you have the nuntaktktkzzzt. I can smell it.
The nodes.
You've altered it.
My Tía. My aunt Selima. She...
Really so naughty that you brought it to the Terrans!
Ktktktktktktkt!
Come, we must talk.
They will take us.
Take us where?!
To Boreale. Underground.

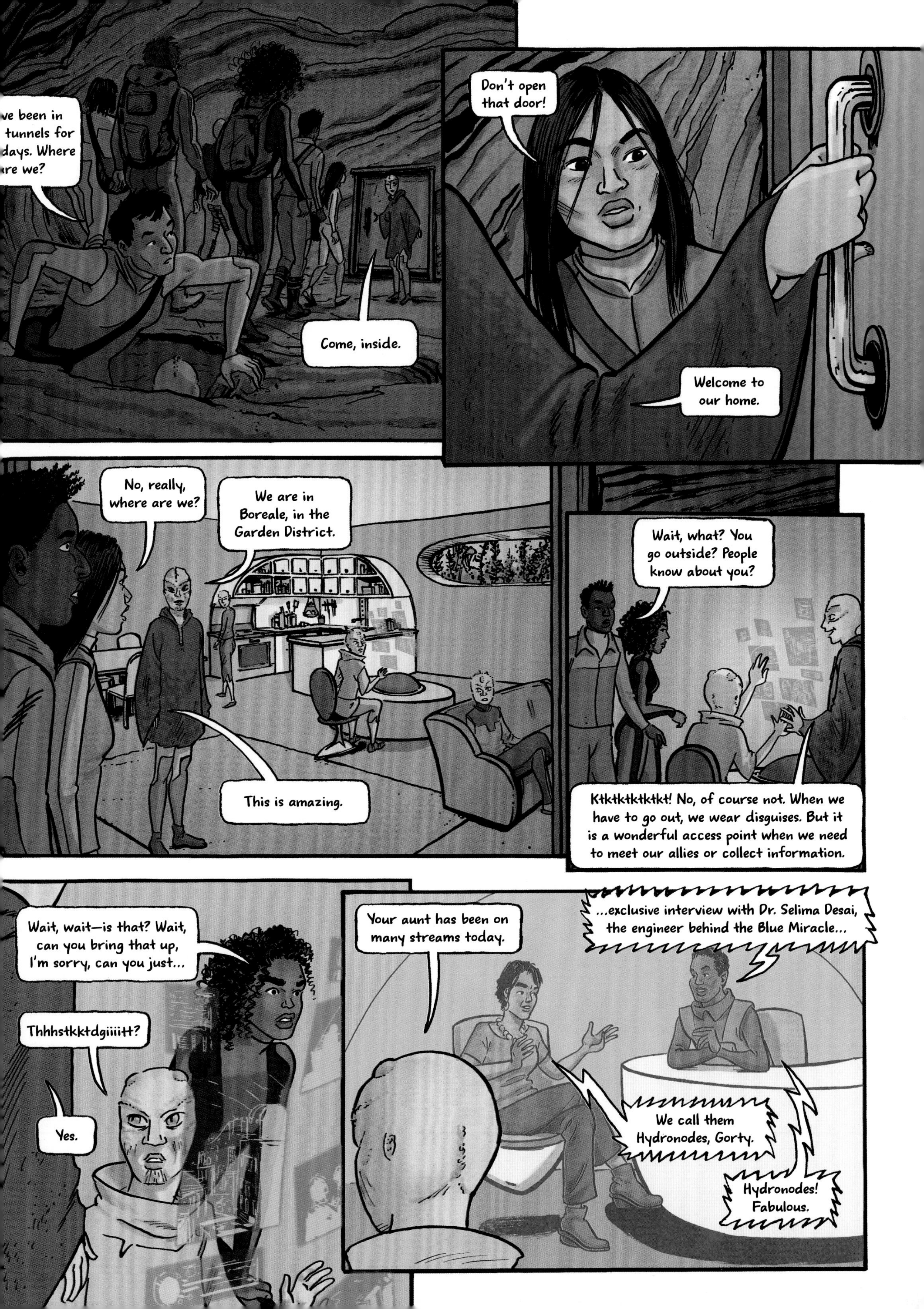

...ve been in
tunnels for
days. Where
are we?
Come, inside.
Don't open
that door!
Welcome to
our home.
No, really,
where are we?
We are in
Boreale, in the
Garden District.
This is amazing.
Wait, what? You
go outside? People
know about you?
Ktktktktktkt! No, of course not. When we have to go out, we wear disguises. But it is a wonderful access point when we need to meet our allies or collect information.
Wait, wait—is that? Wait, can you bring that up, I'm sorry, can you just...
Thhhstkktdgiiiitt?
Yes.
Your aunt has been on many streams today.
...exclusive interview with Dr. Selima Desai, the engineer behind the Blue Miracle...
We call them Hydronodes, Gorty.
Hydronodes! Fabulous.

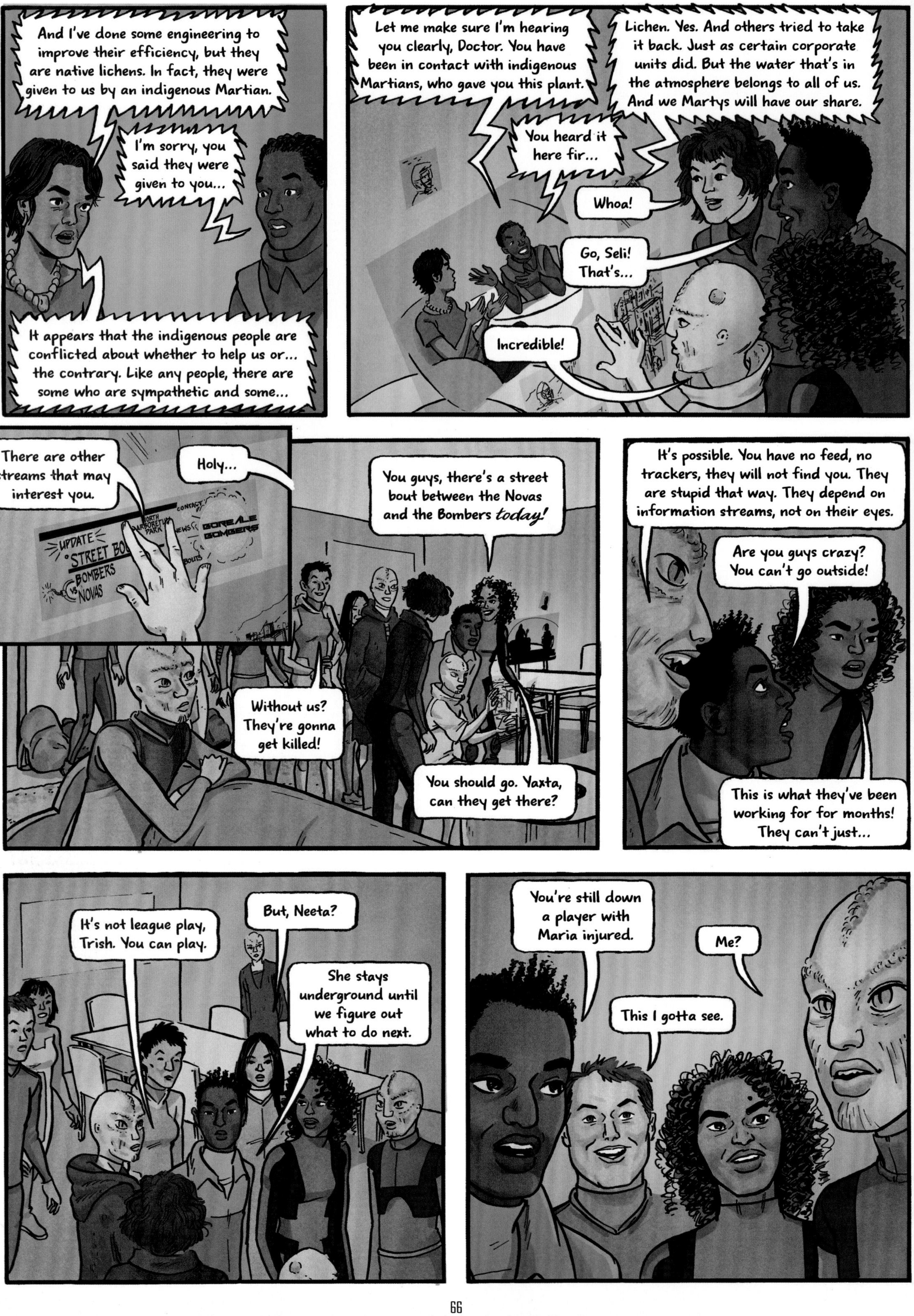
And I've done some engineering to improve their efficiency, but they are native lichens. In fact, they were given to us by an indigenous Martian.
I'm sorry, you said they were given to you...
It appears that the indigenous people are conflicted about whether to help us or... the contrary. Like any people, there are some who are sympathetic and some...
Let me make sure I'm hearing you clearly, Doctor. You have been in contact with indigenous Martians, who gave you this plant.
Lichen. Yes. And others tried to take it back. Just as certain corporate units did. But the water that's in the atmosphere belongs to all of us. And we Martys will have our share.
You heard it here fir...
Whoa!
Go, Seli! That's...
Incredible!
There are other streams that may interest you.
Holy...
UPDATE
BOMBERS
VS
NOVAS
CONTACT
NEWS
BOUTS
BOREALE BOMBERS
You guys, there's a street bout between the Novas and the Bombers *today!*
Without us? They're gonna get killed!
You should go. Yaxta, can they get there?
It's possible. You have no feed, no trackers, they will not find you. They are stupid that way. They depend on information streams, not on their eyes.
Are you guys crazy? You can't go outside!
This is what they've been working for for months! They can't just...
It's not league play, Trish. You can play.
But, Neeta?
She stays underground until we figure out what to do next.
You're still down a player with Maria injured.
Me?
This I gotta see.

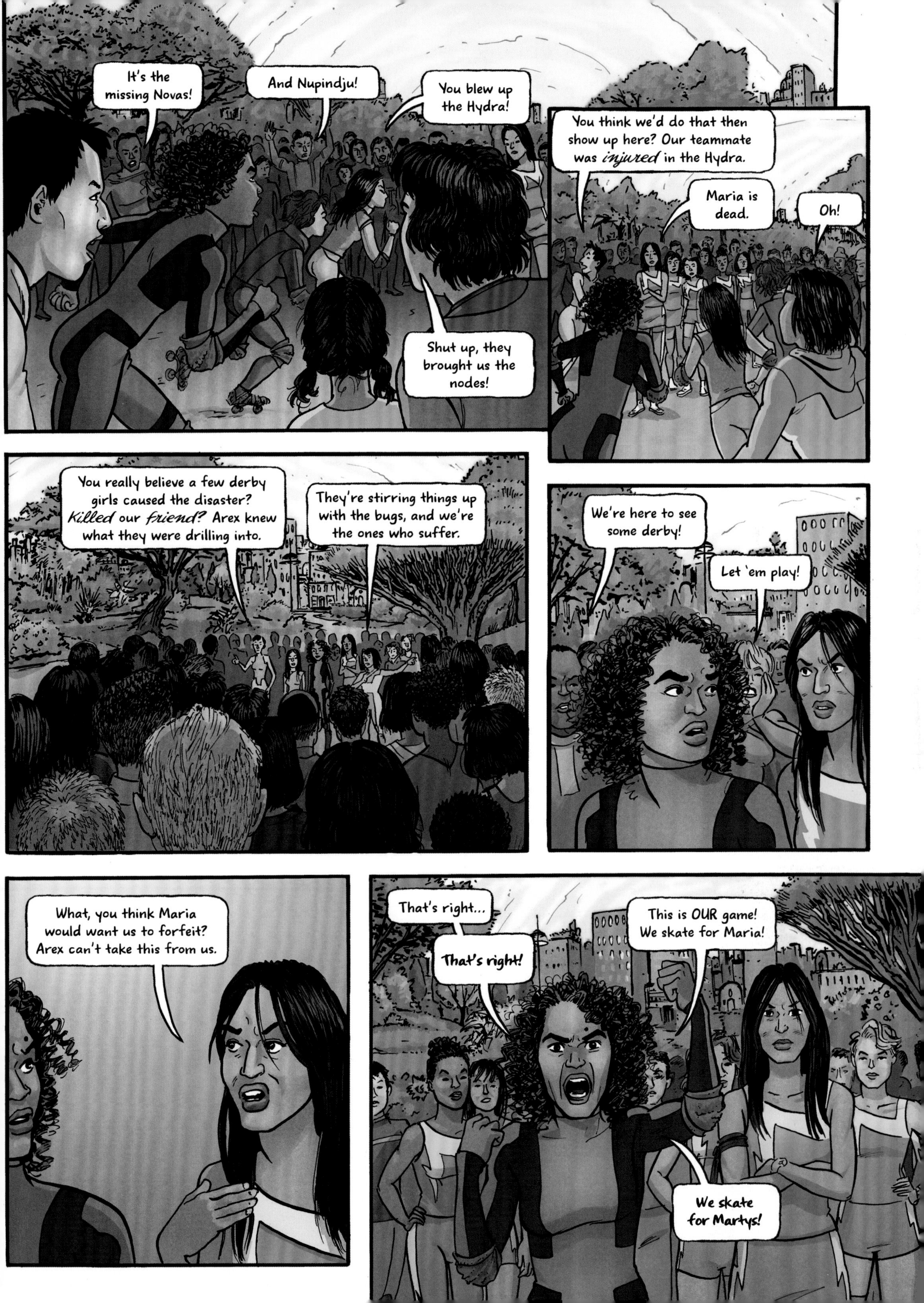
It's the missing Novas!
And Nupindju!
You blew up the Hydra!
Shut up, they brought us the nodes!
You think we'd do that then show up here? Our teammate was *injured* in the Hydra.
Maria is dead.
Oh!
You really believe a few derby girls caused the disaster? *Killed* our *friend?* Arex knew what they were drilling into.
They're stirring things up with the bugs, and we're the ones who suffer.
We're here to see some derby!
Let 'em play!
What, you think Maria would want us to forfeit? Arex can't take this from us.
That's right...
That's right!
This is OUR game! We skate for Maria!
We skate for Martys!

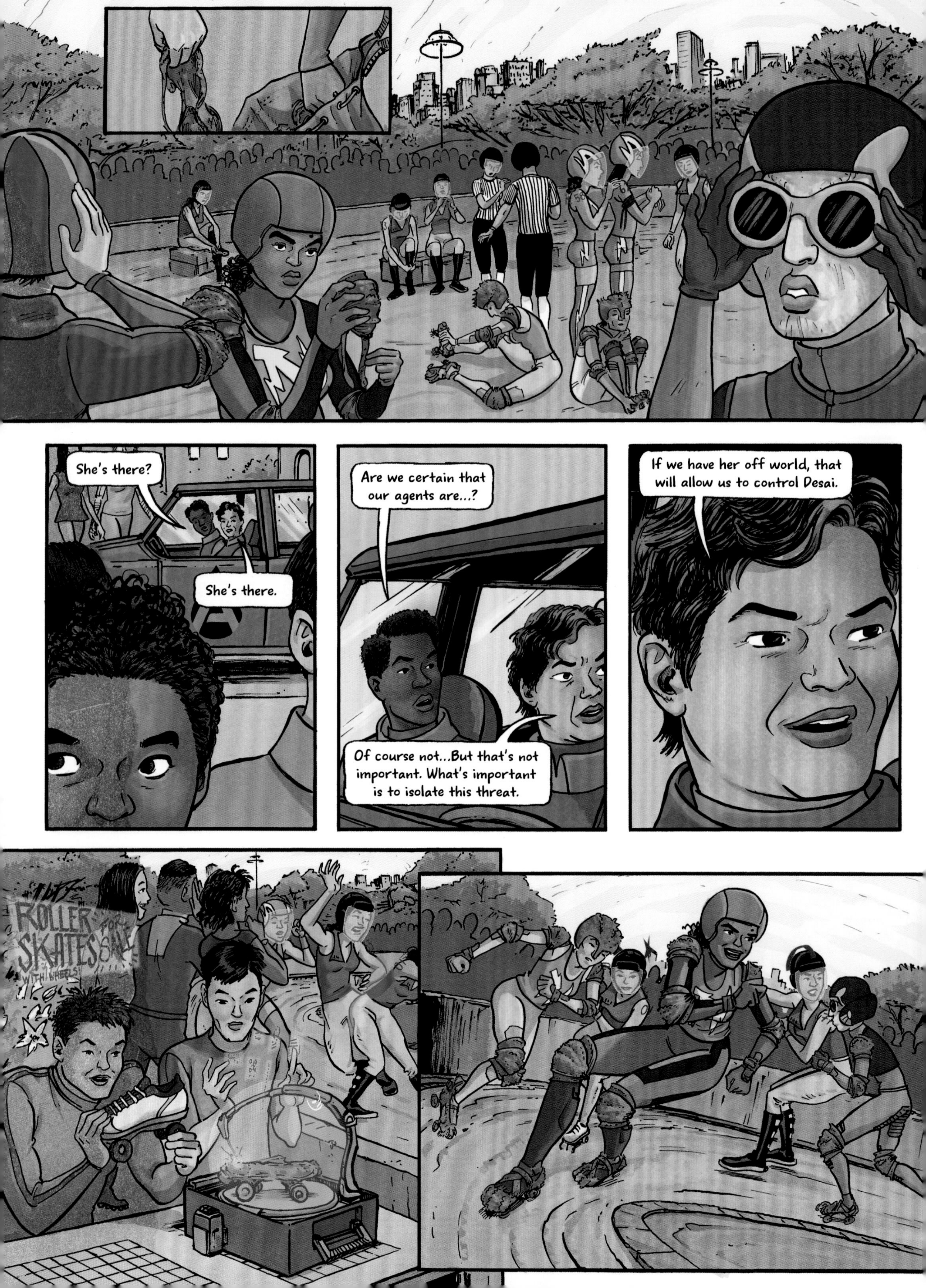

She's there?
She's there.
Are we certain that our agents are...?
Of course not...But that's not important. What's important is to isolate this threat.
If we have her off world, that will allow us to control Desai.
ROLLER SKATES FOR SALE
WITH WHEELS!

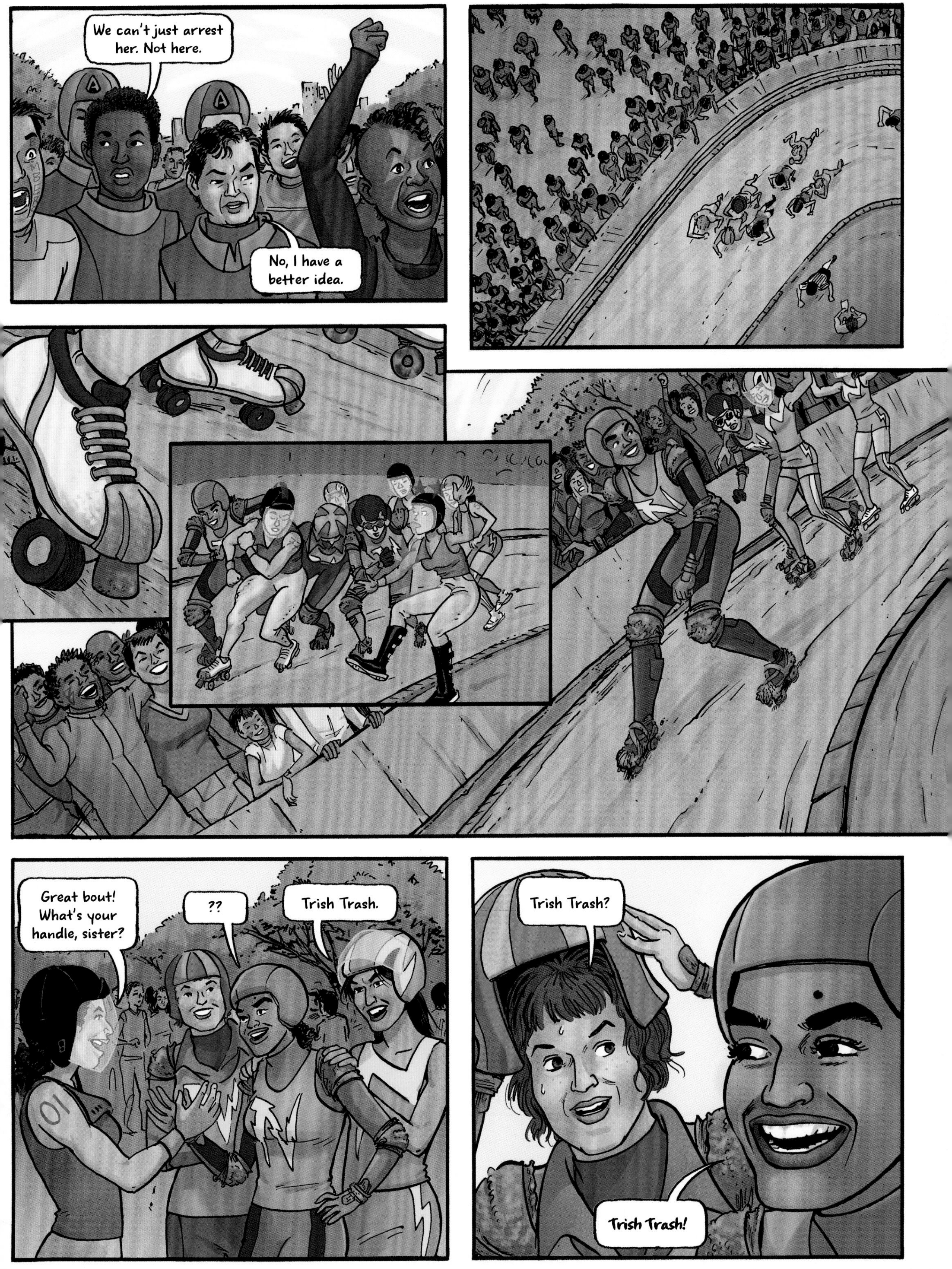
We can't just arrest her. Not here.
No, I have a better idea.
Great bout! What's your handle, sister?
??
Trish Trash.
Trish Trash?
Trish Trash!

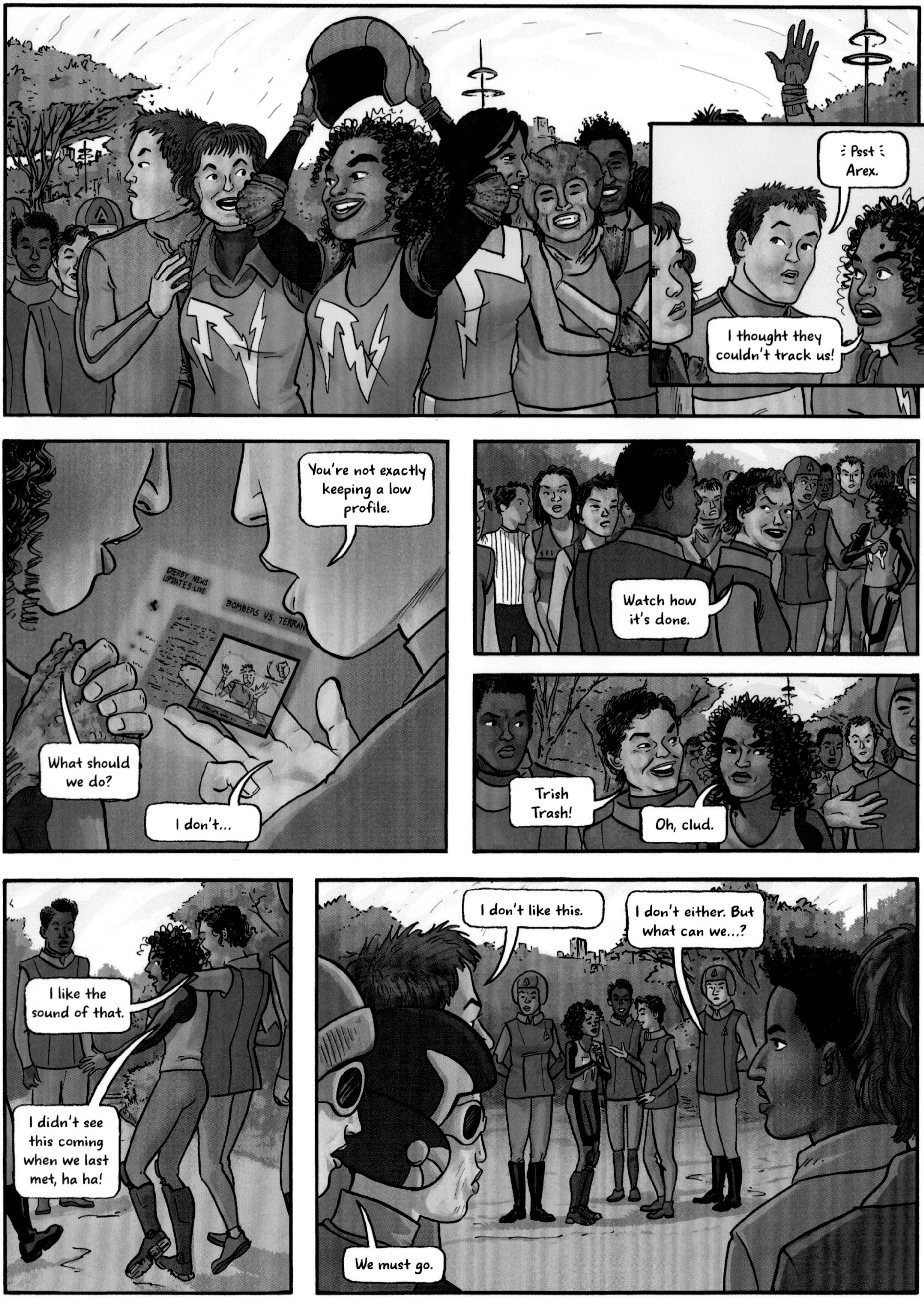

Psst Arex.
I thought they couldn't track us!
You're not exactly keeping a low profile.
DERBY NEWS UPDATES LIVE
BOMBERS VS. TERRAN
What should we do?
I don't...
Watch how it's done.
Trish Trash!
Oh, clud.
I like the sound of that.
I didn't see this coming when we last met, ha ha!
I don't like this.
I don't either. But what can we...?
We must go.

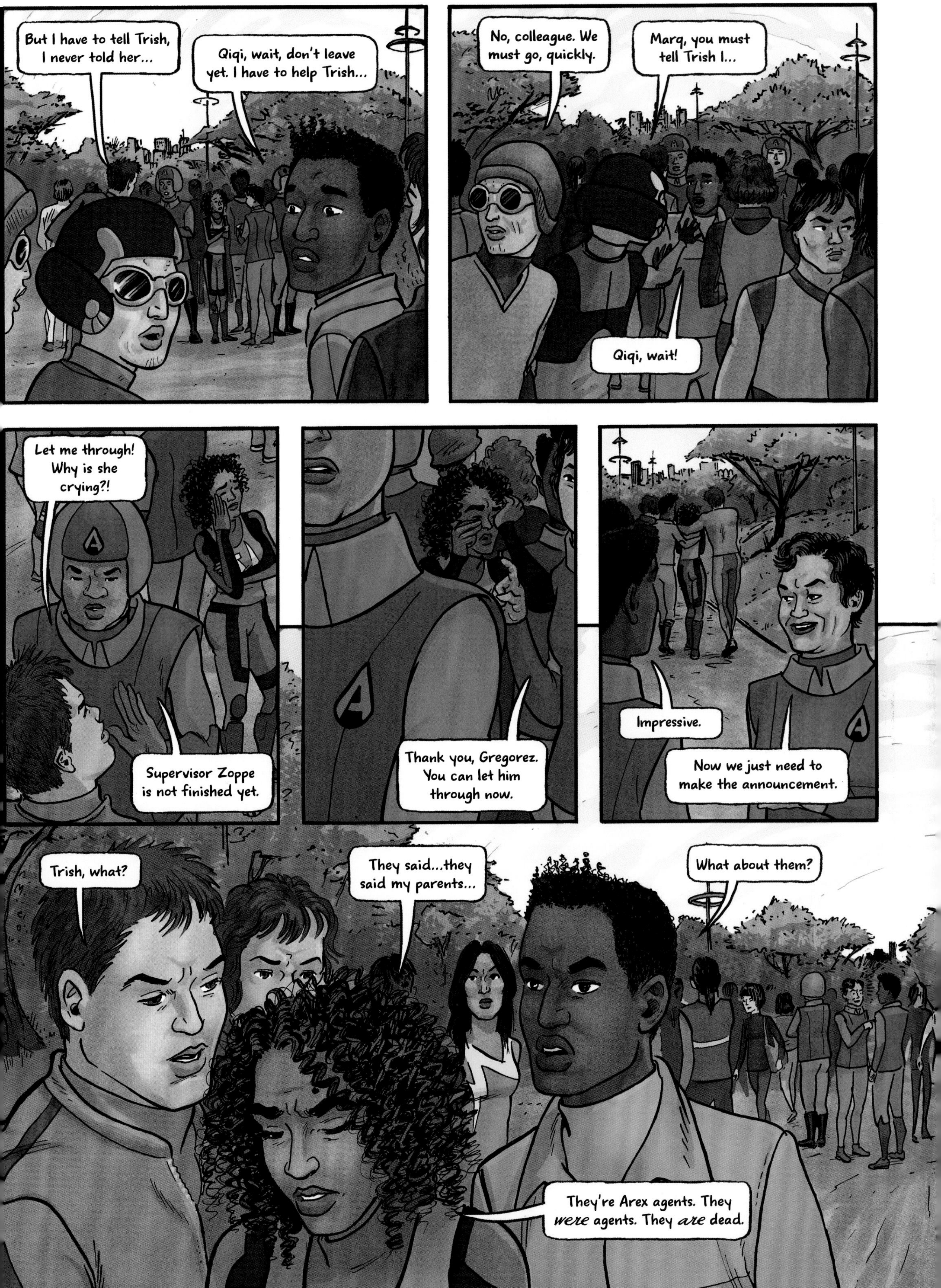
But I have to tell Trish, I never told her…
Qiqi, wait, don't leave yet. I have to help Trish…
No, colleague. We must go, quickly.
Marq, you must tell Trish I…
Qiqi, wait!
Let me through! Why is she crying?!
Supervisor Zoppe is not finished yet.
Thank you, Gregorez. You can let him through now.
Impressive.
Now we just need to make the announcement.
Trish, what?
They said…they said my parents…
What about them?
They're Arex agents. They *were* agents. They *are* dead.

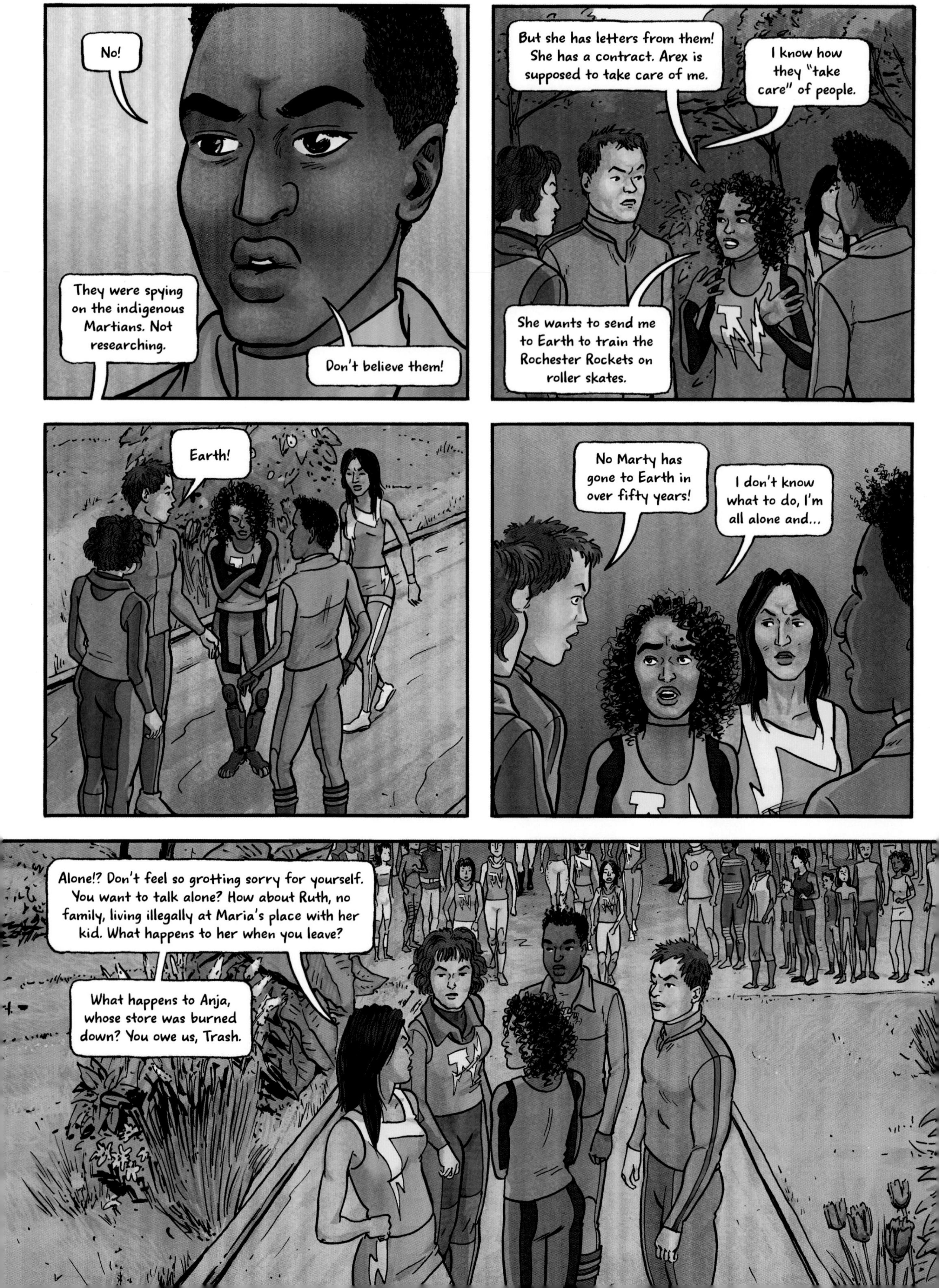
No!
They were spying on the indigenous Martians. Not researching.
Don't believe them!
But she has letters from them! She has a contract. Arex is supposed to take care of me.
I know how they "take care" of people.
She wants to send me to Earth to train the Rochester Rockets on roller skates.
Earth!
No Marty has gone to Earth in over fifty years!
I don't know what to do, I'm all alone and...
Alone!? Don't feel so grotting sorry for yourself. You want to talk alone? How about Ruth, no family, living illegally at Maria's place with her kid. What happens to her when you leave?
What happens to Anja, whose store was burned down? You owe us, Trash.

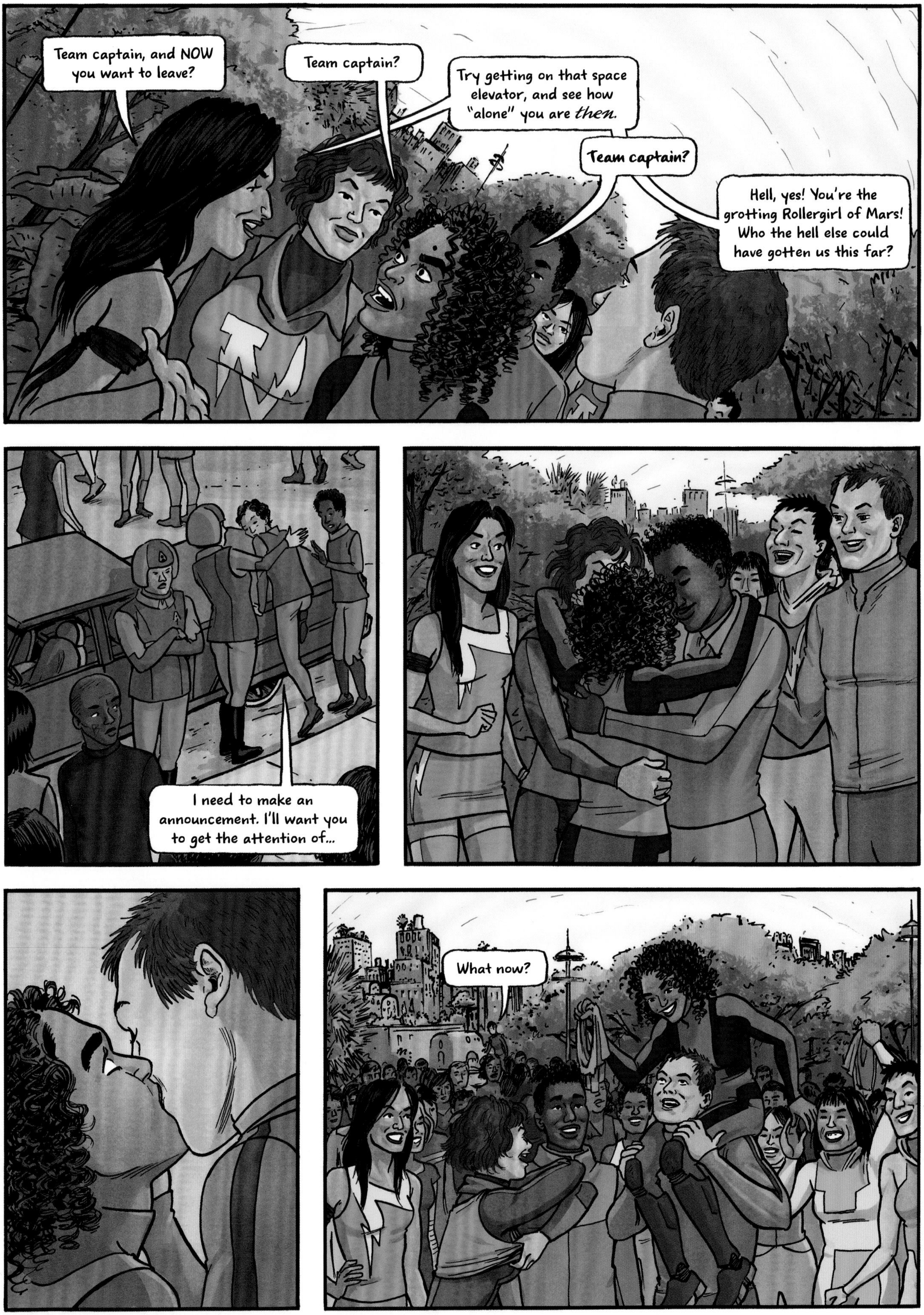
Team captain, and NOW you want to leave?
Team captain?
Try getting on that space elevator, and see how "alone" you are *then.*
Team captain?
Hell, yes! You're the grotting Rollergirl of Mars! Who the hell else could have gotten us this far?
I need to make an announcement. I'll want you to get the attention of...
What now?

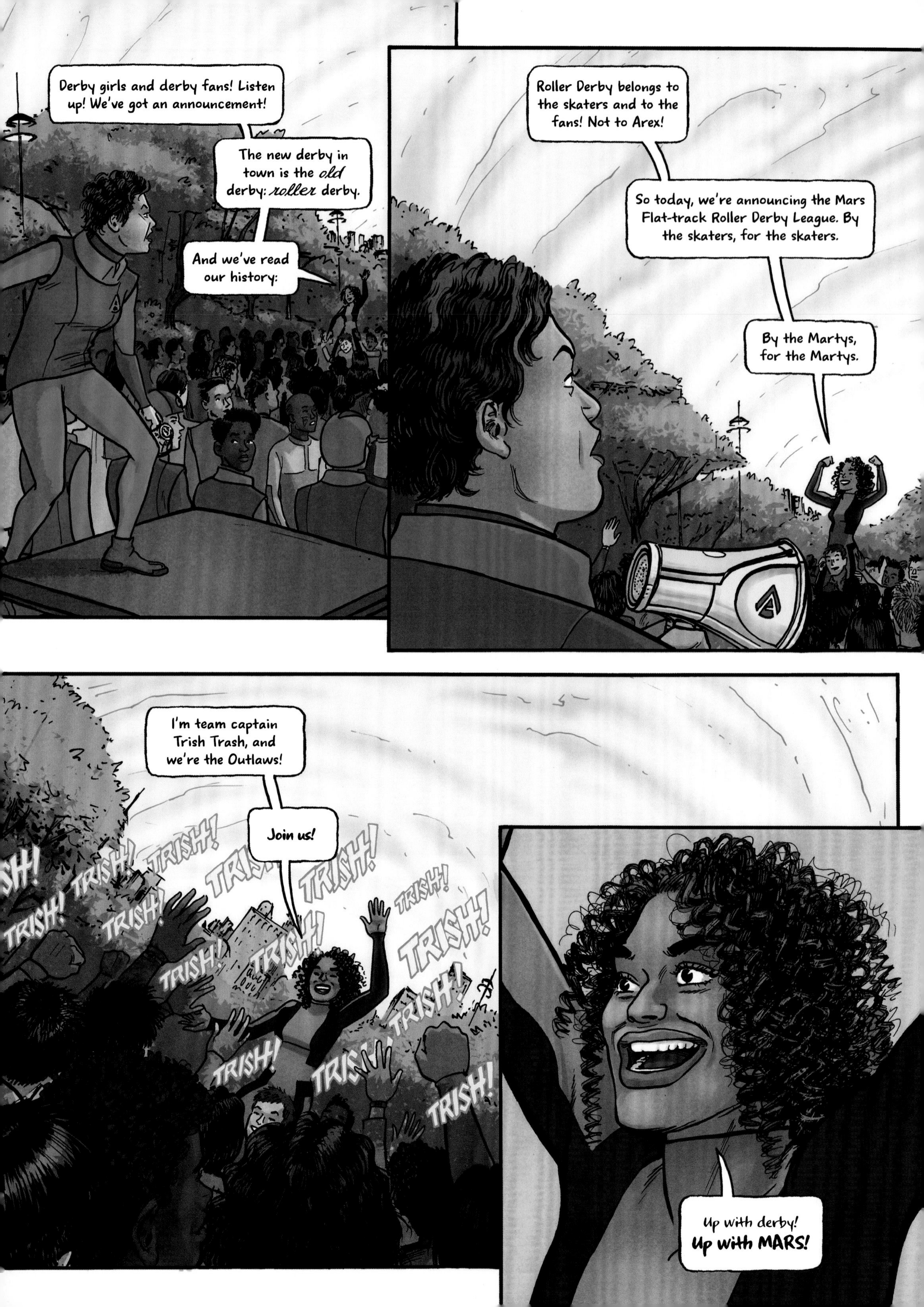
Derby girls and derby fans! Listen up! We've got an announcement!
The new derby in town is the *old* derby: *roller* derby.
And we've read our history:
Roller Derby belongs to the skaters and to the fans! Not to Arex!
So today, we're announcing the Mars Flat-track Roller Derby League. By the skaters, for the skaters.
By the Martys, for the Martys.
I'm team captain Trish Trash, and we're the Outlaws!
Join us!
TRISH! TRISH! TRISH! TRISH! TRISH! TRISH! TRISH! TRISH! TRISH! TRISH! TRISH! TRISH! TRISH!
Up with derby! **Up with MARS!**

If you enjoyed **TRISH TRASH**, you may also enjoy **THE WENDY PROJECT**...

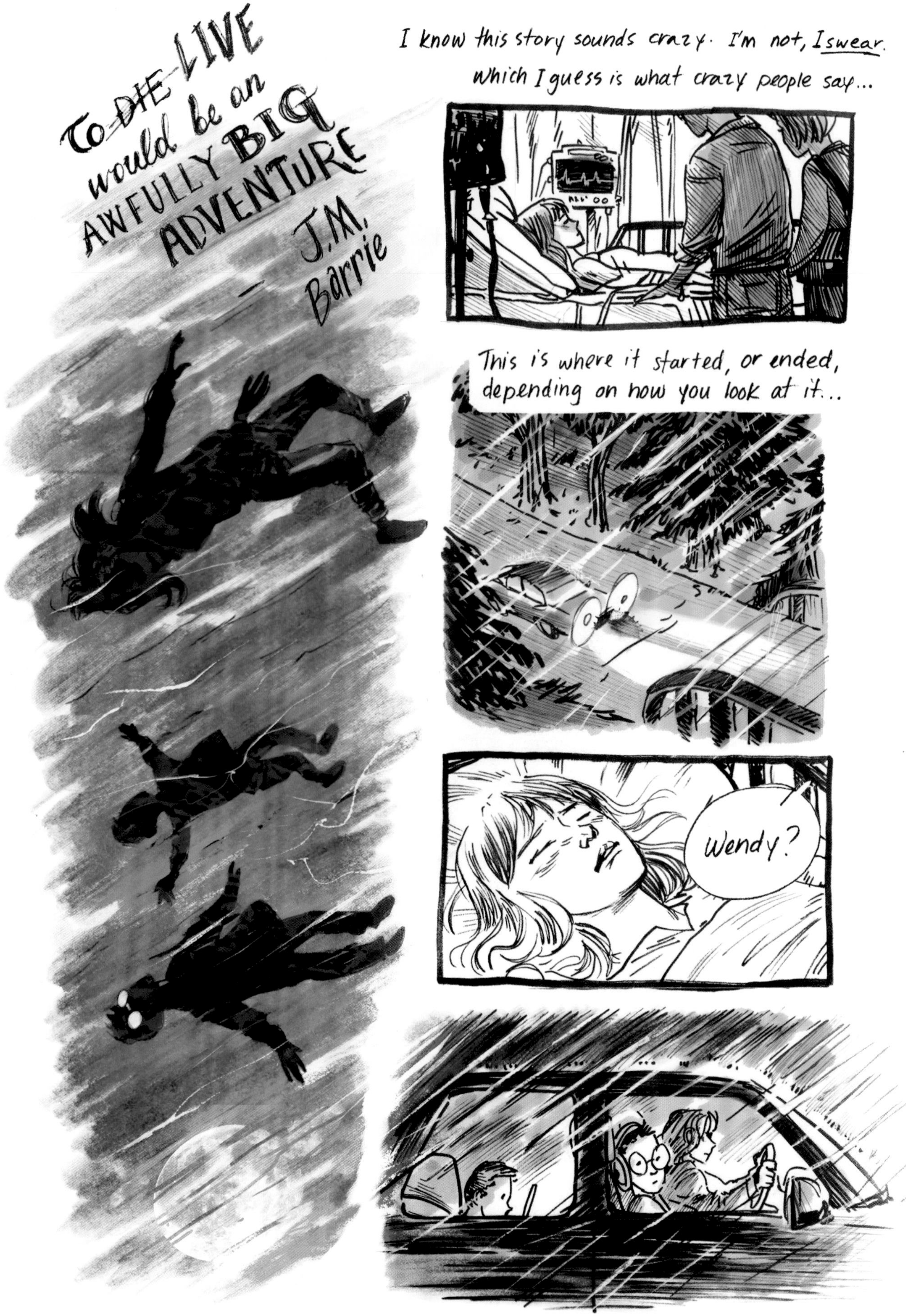
To ~~DIE~~ LIVE would be an AWFULLY BIG ADVENTURE
– J.M. Barrie
I know this story sounds crazy. I'm not, I swear.
Which I guess is what crazy people say...
This is where it started, or ended, depending on how you look at it...
Wendy?

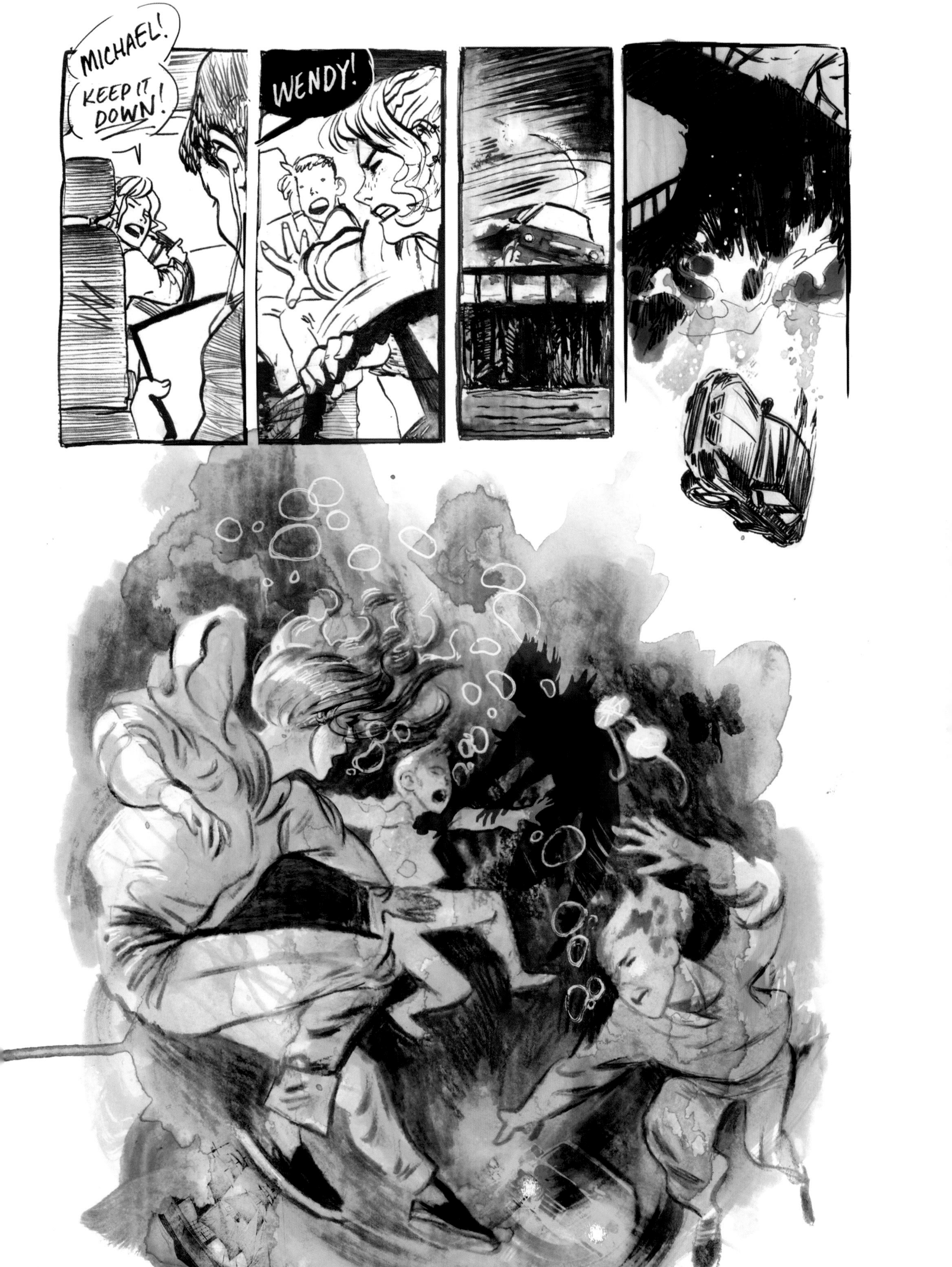
MICHAEL!
KEEP IT DOWN!
WENDY!

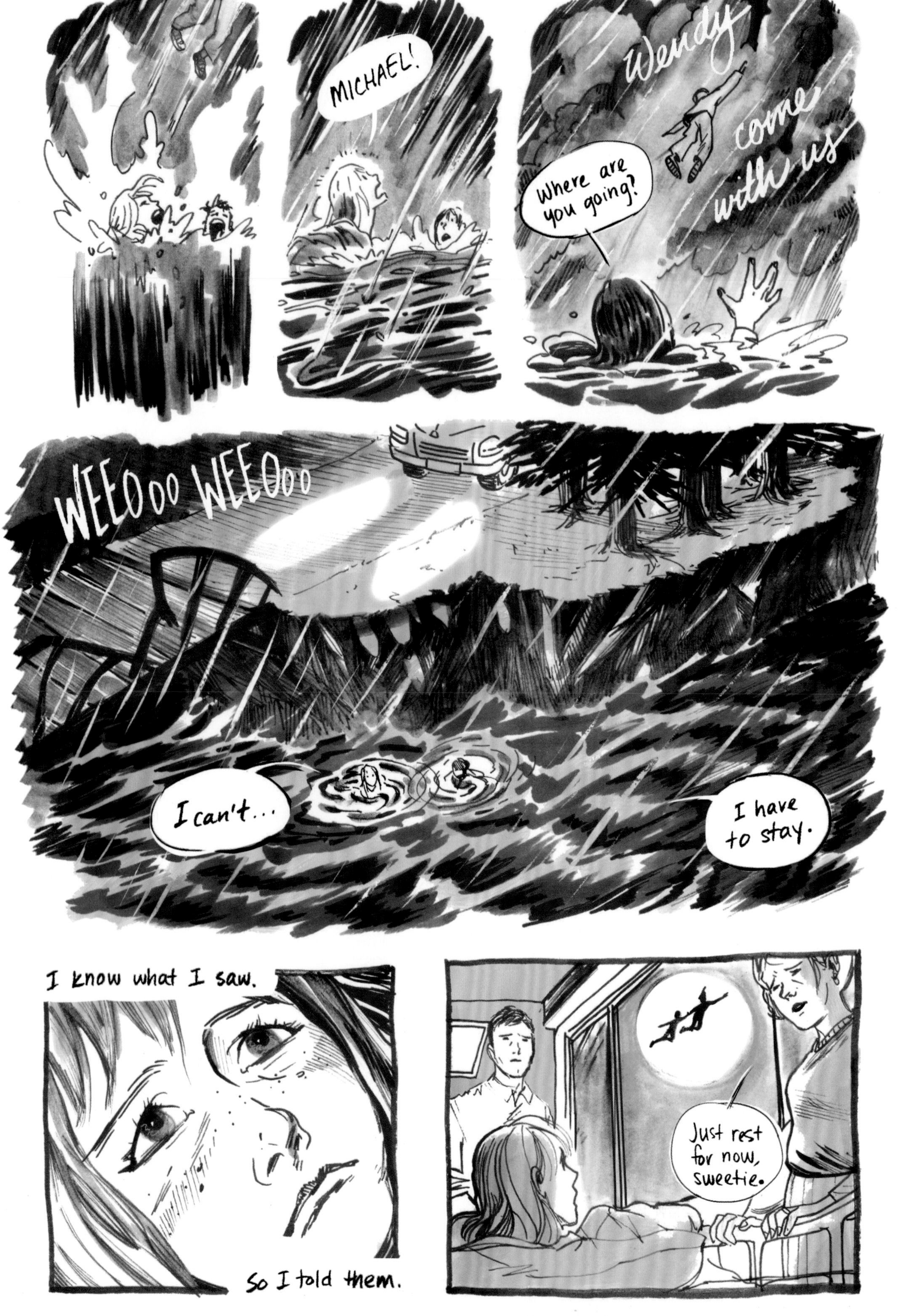
MICHAEL!
Wendy
come with us
Where are you going?
WEEOoo WEEOoo
I can't...
I have to stay.
I know what I saw.
So I told them.
Just rest for now, sweetie.

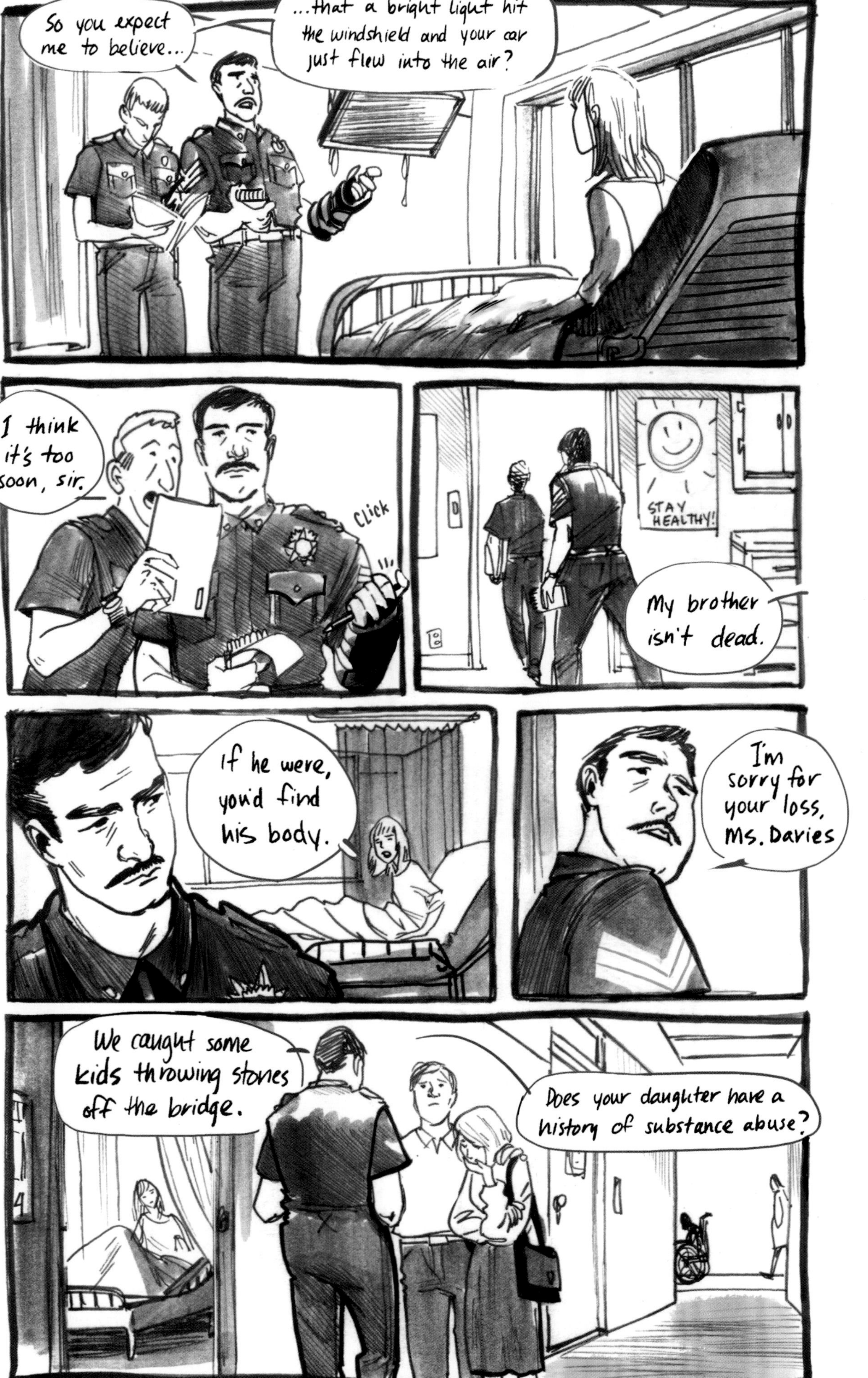
So you expect me to believe...
...that a bright light hit the windshield and your car just flew into the air?
I think it's too soon, sir.
CLICK
STAY HEALTHY!
My brother isn't dead.
If he were, you'd find his body.
I'm sorry for your loss, Ms. Davies
We caught some kids throwing stones off the bridge.
Does your daughter have a history of substance abuse?

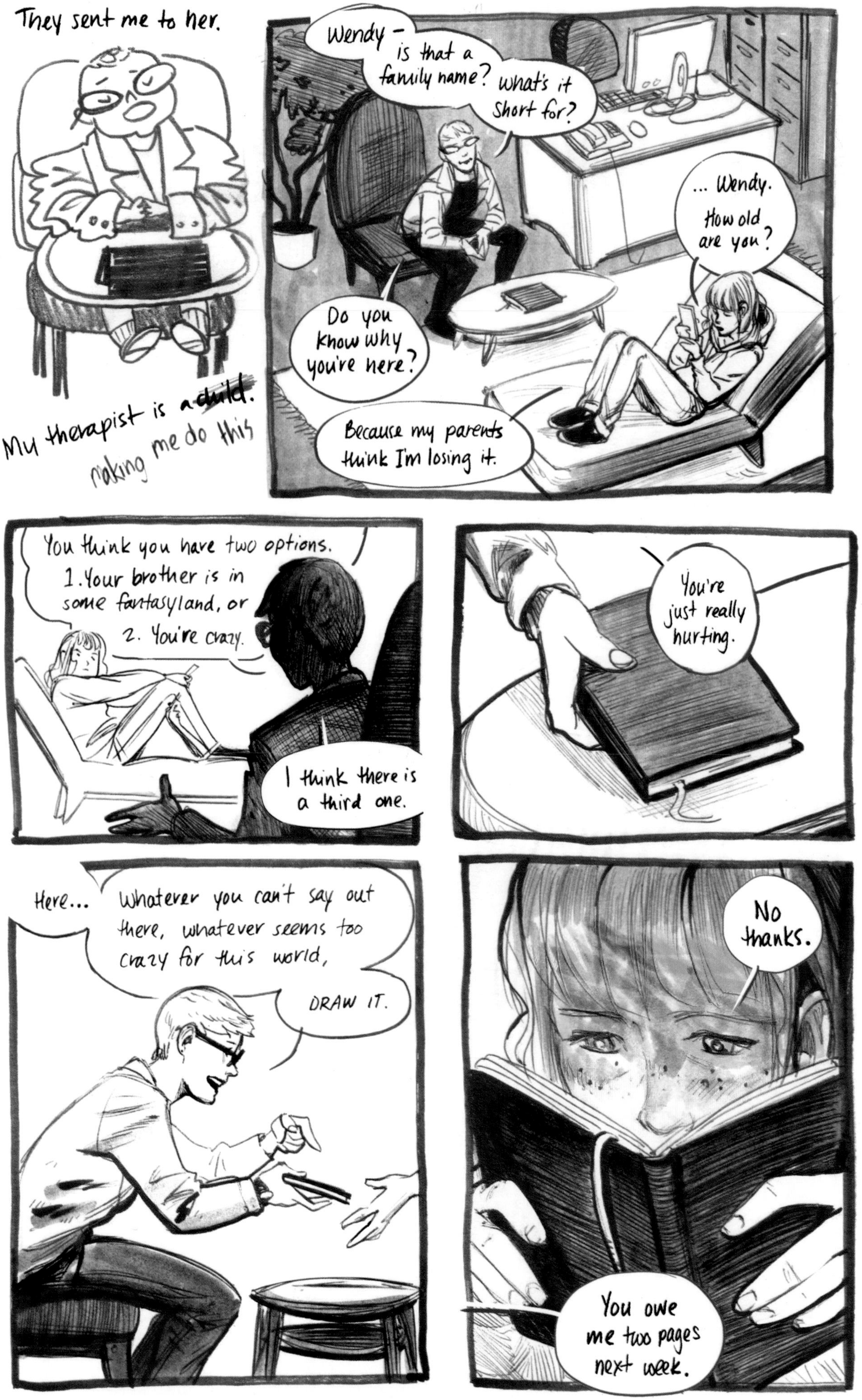
They sent me to her.
Wendy - is that a family name? what's it short for?
... Wendy. How old are you?
Do you know why you're here?
Because my parents think I'm losing it.
My therapist is a child. making me do this
You think you have two options. 1. Your brother is in some fantasyland, or 2. You're crazy.
I think there is a third one.
You're just really hurting.
Here...
Whatever you can't say out there, whatever seems too crazy for this world,
DRAW IT.
No thanks.
You owe me two pages next week.